**"The person who killed my sister is still out there and my niece is still missing. If we find the real killer, he'll be able to tell us where her baby is."**

Thomas put his hand on Molly's arm. Molly felt a warm flush move through her body as she stared into his hazel eyes. How long had it been since she'd been moved by a touch? She didn't even want to think about it.

"I'm going to make you a promise, Molly Harper," Thomas said, his voice warm but steely. "We're going to find Kate and bring her home to you. No matter what we have to do to find her."

"Meow!" Familiar jumped on Molly's lap and put his paw on top of Thomas's hand.

# CAROLINE BURNES

# FAMILIAR ESCAPE

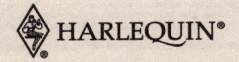

**HARLEQUIN®**

TORONTO • NEW YORK • LONDON
AMSTERDAM • PARIS • SYDNEY • HAMBURG
STOCKHOLM • ATHENS • TOKYO • MILAN • MADRID
PRAGUE • WARSAW • BUDAPEST • AUCKLAND

ISBN 0-373-88679-9

FAMILIAR ESCAPE

This edition published by arrangement with Harlequin Books S.A.

® and TM are trademarks of the publisher. Trademarks indicated with ® are registered in the United States Patent and Trademark Office, the Canadian Trade Marks Office and in other countries.

www.eHarlequin.com

**Printed in U.S.A.**

## Books by Caroline Burnes

FEAR FAMILIAR

Don't miss any of our special offers. Write to us at the
following address for information on our newest releases.

Harlequin Reader Service
U.S.: 3010 Walden Ave., P.O. Box 1325, Buffalo, NY 14269
Canadian: P.O. Box 609, Fort Erie, Ont. L2A 5X3

Fifteen years ago a young black kitten
was left in a carrier at my door. I named him
E. A. Poe, and his intelligence and personality
figured prominently in the creation of
Familiar, the black cat detective. Poe died
this year, leaving a huge hole in my life.
This book is for him. E. A. Poe, 1990-2005.
To steal a line from Owen Meany,
"Into paradise may the angels lead you."

# Chapter One

This is one sad-looking group of felons. Since I'm being paid for my assessment of Thomas Lakeman, I need to use all my powers of observation. Is Thomas a murderer and a kidnapper? That's what I shall try to ascertain.

Though I prefer to focus my attention on the fairer sex, especially the babes with long legs and curves in all the right places like my current employer, I'm going to check out Thomas and see what my sixth feline sense tells me about him.

Thomas is charged with murdering his friend and neighbor, Anna Harper Goodman, and then abducting a nine-month-old baby girl, Kate. Anna's body was found in Thomas's home, but there was no sign of the baby girl.

That was five days ago, and no one had found even a good clue to the whereabouts of the baby until yesterday. That's when I got

*the call that put me on a flight out to Jeffer-
son, Texas, to help Molly Harper hunt for
her missing niece.*

*Molly opened her mail to find a typewrit-
ten note claiming that baby Kate is alive.
After four days of believing that both Anna
and Kate were dead, Molly suddenly has
hope that her infant niece can be found.*

*My professional opinion of the note is that
it's real, but there's also the possibility that
it's some kind of cruel hoax. If Thomas
Lakeman, the quiet man sitting on the end of
the bench there is the killer, Molly and I hope
to be able to convince him to tell us what he
did with the baby.*

*Ah, Thomas sees me. His pale hazel eyes
hold curiosity and intelligence, and a hint
of…kindness? Not exactly the qualities I'd
ascribe to a killer. At any rate, he's very
aware that I'm interested in him, and I have
to hand it to him, he's not stupid enough to
call to me. Anyone with two brain cells knows
cats never come when called. Thomas must
be experienced with the superior species of
felines, or he could simply be intellectually
superior to most humanoids. Whichever it is,
he's a cool customer. He's merely staring at
me and waiting for me to make the first move.*

*From my vantage point inside the jail, I can see Thomas and Molly. Even worried and frustrated, Molly is a beautiful woman. She has the look of an artist with her straight, dark hair and serious gray eyes. From what I heard, Anna looked a lot like her, just a few years older. A few years older and light-years different, from what Molly has told me about her sister.*

*I believe exploring those differences will help us find the baby, if little Kate is still alive.*

*I'm walking over to Thomas. It's a test. The other men sitting on the bench waiting to be returned to their cells either ignore me or leer at me in a way that says they want to hurt me. For some reason, cats excite the blood lust of lower animal forms like them. I'm careful to stay out of their reach. I also have to keep an eye out for the jailers. I'm not exactly an invited guest here at the county lockup.*

*Thomas maintains eye contact as he reaches down to me. He's stroking my back, not attempting to pick me up. He's rubbing my head. The man has a way with cats! His hands are leathery from outdoor work, but his touch is gentle. Not at all what I expected.*

*Uh-oh, here comes the deputy. I'd better scoot out of sight and listen in.*

MOLLY HARPER CLUTCHED the slip of paper in her hand and paced. Ten steps forward, reverse, then back. She'd been waiting over an hour, now, to speak with a deputy. As far as she could tell, the welfare of her infant niece wasn't a high priority on anyone's list.

Texas justice, that legendary commodity associated with the Texas Rangers, didn't seem to apply to state residents who weighed only twenty pounds! She fumed as she paced, the heels of her leather boots tapping along the cement floor of the county lockup.

She caught a glimpse of Familiar, as the black cat detective she'd hired to help her darted past the doorway to the jail. The cat had come highly recommended to her.

Just as the cat disappeared, she heard the jangle of keys.

"Miss Harper?"

She turned to face a slender deputy. "I'd like to speak to Thomas Lakeman."

The deputy frowned. "You should wait until the trial."

Her anger spiked. "I don't have time to wait! My niece may be dying as we stand here discussing this. I want to talk to him and I want to talk to him now."

The deputy's face had grown stony. "He

doesn't have to speak with you. Even though his lawyer has agreed for you to talk to him, Lakeman doesn't have to say a word to you."

"Can you at least ask him?"

"It could take a while."

"Listen, Officer, if I find out that this delay has caused harm to my niece, I'll make sure the newspapers know your name."

The deputy turned and walked away. Molly paced the room again, hoping that Familiar was having better luck than she.

"Miss Harper?"

She turned to find the same deputy standing in the doorway. "Yes?"

"Mr. Lakeman has agreed to see you. Please follow me."

Molly was shocked that Thomas Lakeman had agreed to talk to her, but she didn't hesitate as she followed the deputy to a small room with a table and two chairs facing each other across it.

"Thank you," she said as she took a seat and waited for the man accused of killing her sister to be brought to her.

NOT EVEN the institutional green of the walls could sallow the woman's complexion. Thomas followed the deputy into the room, aware that Molly Harper was one of the love-liest women he'd ever encountered. She looked a lot like her sister, Anna, but there was something more to Molly. Her skin glowed and her hair was lustrous. She had the same coloring as her sister, but Molly seemed luminous, as if some inner light gave her a unique glow. There was also a fire in her eyes that scalded him.

He felt the anger and hatred as he sat across from her. He dropped his gaze to the scarred surface of the table and wondered if his lawyer, Bradley Alain, had been on target when he recommended that Thomas talk with her. Bradley felt that if he cooperated with Molly, she might help Thomas as a character witness at his trial. With all the evidence against him, he didn't know if he'd be able to convince her that he was innocent of killing her sister. The only role he'd ever played in Anna's life was that of friend and co-worker. It had been his home that Anna came to whenever she was afraid of her husband's rages, his fists.

The deputy locked Thomas's handcuffs to a chain that came up from the floor. "This is Molly Harper," the deputy said. "Don't do anything foolish." He stepped back to a corner of the room to allow them as much privacy as he could.

"Where is Kate?" Molly asked.

The question was spoken with such controlled fury that he looked up. "I don't know." It was the truth and the only thing he could say. If he had any inkling where the baby had been taken, he'd tell. The sheriff was convinced that Kate was dead. So convinced, in fact, that no law enforcement agency was even hunting for the baby.

"I have some savings." She spoke in a way that told him she'd rehearsed this. "I'm willing to give you everything I have. You can hire a celebrity lawyer or do whatever you want with the money. Just give me back my niece."

Though her anger was daunting, her pain was even more difficult to bear. "I'm sorry," he said. "I don't know where Kate is. I had nothing to do with any of this."

"My sister's body was found at your house. How can you claim to be innocent?"

Across the table from him she was trembling so that her bracelet tapped against the table. "I was camping that night. I wasn't home. I had no idea your sister was at my house."

"How did she get inside?"

He'd told this story to the deputies, but no one believed him. Still, he had to try again. "Anna had a key to my house. There were times she needed a place to go." He hesitated. How much should he tell this angry woman about the abuse her sister suffered?

"She told me she had a friend, a safe place to go." Molly had gained control of her shaking. "She never said a name, only that the person was a friend."

"Then you knew she had difficulty in her marriage."

Molly started to rise, but when the deputy came over, she sat back down. "Darwin hit her. I know that. I begged her to leave him. I sent her money to get out, but Anna wouldn't leave. She used the money for a down payment on a house."

Thomas nodded. "I know. She told me about the money you sent and how generous you were. She named you as beneficiary. She knew you'd take care of Kate. Anna was convinced she could change Darwin, but just in case, she took legal precautions to protect herself and your investment."

"She believed that somehow it was her fault, that she brought the beatings on," Molly said, turning her face away. "I never cared about the money. I should have come over here and taken her and the baby no matter what she said."

"Anna was a grown woman. She had a right to make her own choices, even if they were wrong." He wanted to comfort this woman. "Hindsight is twenty-twenty, Miss Harper. Understand there was nothing you could have done. Believe me, I tried."

She turned to look at him, this time her pain unshielded by her anger. "You tried to convince her to leave, didn't you?"

"More than once. She wouldn't hear of it. While she was pregnant with Kate, he didn't hit her. She thought the baby would change him, would make him love her. I gave her a key to my place so that she'd have somewhere safe to go if it got bad again. That's how she got into my house. What happened after that, I don't know."

"If you were camping, surely the police could prove it?"

He thought about what she was asking. For the first time there was a glimmer of hope that she might be willing to at least listen to his side of the story. "They did prove I had set up camp. They found my gear and things where I said they were, but the witnesses who knew I was at my camp all night have disappeared. The police say I established the campsite as an alibi and then drove back to town to kill Anna."

"She was shot with your gun."

It was an accusation. "I know. The gun was in a bedside table. I kept it there for protection."

"I would have thought you'd take it with you camping."

"The things I'm afraid of aren't in the wilderness." The look she gave him was more curious than angry, encouraging him to continue. "I told Anna about the gun. I wanted her to know where it was in case she ever needed to defend herself, or Kate. I always left it there. For her."

"And the motive? The police are saying you loved Anna and when she wouldn't leave Darwin, you killed her."

He shook his head. "I did love Anna, but not in the romantic sense. I loved her as a friend. We were close. She was…fragile. We worked together, and somehow I became something akin to an older brother, yet not family." He knew this would hurt, but he had to say it. "She was so ashamed of what her life had become. She didn't want her real family to know how bad it was, how much she endured. But she could talk to me. I didn't judge her. I listened, and when I could, I helped her."

He wasn't certain how Molly Harper was reacting to his words. She was listening, though, and that was further than he'd gotten with anyone else. "She talked about you a lot." He wanted to reach out and touch her hand, to offer comfort, but he didn't. "She admired you so much, even though you were the younger sister. She told me all about you. How brave you were, and strong. She felt she lacked those qualities."

Molly's tears slipped down her cheeks. She made no effort to wipe them away. "Anna never saw herself the way I did. To me she was my big sister. She taught me to dance and to fix my hair. She helped me pick out the dress for my high school prom. She always had time for me."

"She had time for everyone. That was her gift," Thomas said. "That's what made her special."

"Who would kill her?"

"I don't have an answer for you. Not yet." This was a question he'd thought about since his arrest five days ago. The first suspect was

Anna's husband, Darwin Goodman. But the police had interrogated and released him. Darwin had an alibi for the time of the murder. That didn't clear him in Thomas's book—and at his arraignment Thomas had made a big scene accusing Darwin of killing Anna—but why would even a wife-beater like Darwin abduct and hide his own child if Kate was alive? He would have had legal custody of Kate. He didn't have to steal her.

"Did she ever mention anyone else who might want to hurt her?"

He'd given this a lot of thought also. "No. Anna made friends easily, though she didn't let many people close. She did her job and went home to her family. Kate was in day care during the day, and Anna sometimes stopped by my place with the baby after she'd picked her up. She was always headed home to make dinner. Everything seemed routine, up until the evening before she was killed."

"What happened?"

"She and Darwin had another fight. She showed up on my doorstep with Kate. Darwin hadn't hit her, but he'd threatened her. It was the first time she even talked about leaving him."

"But she went back home."

He nodded.

"The police have cleared Darwin."

"I know, but that doesn't make it a fact. They've accused me and I didn't do it."

"Do you have any other suspects?"

He hesitated before he answered. In some ways, it would be easier for her to believe he'd done it and was going to be punished than to think that her sister's murderer was still at large. "I wish I could tell you who did it. I can only tell you that it wasn't me."

Molly rose. "A jury will determine your guilt or innocence, Mr. Lakeman."

"To be honest, Miss Harper, I'm not nearly as worried about my guilt as I am about that little baby girl. The police never found her body. They're basing their conclusions on evidence that led them to the river. But I don't find the evidence conclusive. Kate could be alive."

That stopped her. Her fists clenched and she leaned toward him.

"If you know something, tell me now."

"I was camping that night. There was another couple there, John and Judy. I don't remember their last names. But they were there. We played cards for a while, they drank a few beers and I had coffee. I got a headache and went to bed. When I woke up at five-thirty, they were gone."

"What does that have to do with Kate?"

He could hear the frustration in her voice, and he knew if he didn't make her understand, she would leave.

"If you can find those campers who'll verify my alibi, then you can clear me. I'll help you hunt for Kate." He leaned closer. "If you think there's a prayer your niece is alive, let me help you find her."

She stepped back from the table. "I can't split my time trying to clear your name. I have to focus on finding Kate."

"She is alive, isn't she?" Thomas asked. He could read the truth on her face. Molly Harper wasn't used to lying or even faking the truth. "How do you know she's alive?"

She shook her head. "You can't, or won't, help me." Molly moved to the door of the room. "Deputy, I'm finished here."

She was almost out the door when he called out to her. "Go to the campsite. Carrillo Pass Park. There's a lake. I was on the west side of the lake beside a stand of oaks. John and Judy were camped twenty yards to the right of my tent. Check it out."

Then she was gone, passing the deputy

who would unhook him from the chair and lead him back to the cell where he'd remain until his trial began.

MOLLY ENTERED the corridor and was startled by the black cat. He'd obviously been sitting beside the door, listening to the entire conversation. He followed behind her as she left the jail and went to the parking lot for her Jeep. She was trying hard not to cry. Against all odds, she'd pinned her hopes on the fact that Thomas Lakeman would tell her what had happened to Kate.

She got in the Jeep and leaned against the steering wheel, gathering her ragged courage and any scrap of hope she could muster. She had to keep believing the baby was okay. She had to keep hunting. She couldn't give up.

She pulled the note from her pocket. "The baby is alive. Don't stop hunting, but don't go to the police."

"Meow!" The cat tapped the glove box.

In the few hours she'd been with Familiar, she'd learned to respond to several of his commands. She opened the glove box and watched as he ruffled through some papers. What tumbled out were several maps. He found the one he wanted and presented it to her with a few teeth marks in it.

"It's the local map," she said, opening it up. "What?"

Familiar seemed to study the map before he put his black paw on Carrillo Pass Park.

"Meow!" It was more of a command than a request.

"You've got to be kidding." She looked at him. "You want to follow up Thomas Lakeman's cockamamie idea that I validate his alibi?"

Familiar's green eyes blinked twice.

"It's a waste of our time."

He put his paw on the map and extended his claws. When he removed his paw there were several holes surrounding the state park. He batted the keys dangling in the ignition.

"I hope you know what you're doing," she said as she started the engine and aimed the car toward the highway that would take them to Carrillo Pass.

It wasn't as if she had any other leads to follow. She'd give the cat an hour to satisfy his curiosity, and then she'd do what she should have done in the first place—turn the note over to the authorities.

## Chapter Two

The only good thing about being back in his cell was that they removed the handcuffs. Thomas sat on the thin bunk mattress and tried not to hear the sounds of the other incarcerated men or to think about the future. For just one second, he'd thought he might have connected with Molly Harper. That had given him hope—and hope was the only thing he couldn't afford.

Someone had framed him, and done a professional job of it. Someone who knew of his friendship with Anna Goodman. Someone who knew she had a key to his home and access to his gun.

Since the terrible morning when the deputies had come to the park and arrested him, Thomas's life had become a nightmare. He'd gleaned enough details about Anna's murder to be able to imagine what had occurred. He could only hope that his imagination was worse than the reality.

In his mind he saw Anna running across his lawn, using her key to unlock his door. She had Kate in her arms, and they were both crying. Anna kept looking back over her shoulder, terrified that someone had followed her. Her fingers fumbled the key as she tried to open the door.

Thomas stopped his thoughts. He couldn't bear to see Anna so afraid, and the one person she was most afraid of was her husband, Darwin. He paced the small cell. The worst curse in the world would be to love the person you feared the most. Anna's relationship with Darwin had been pure hell. Yet she had acted as if she were powerless to change it.

Unless on the night of her murder, she'd intended to take the baby and leave.

He saw her again, putting Kate on his bed as she got the gun from the drawer. She turned and faced the doorway, determined to defend herself against whoever was after her. The bedroom door flew open and—

Thomas grasped the bars and bit back the curse that wanted to escape. Someone had hurt Anna while he was sitting around a campfire drinking coffee and playing cards. And then that someone had framed him.

Now he was helpless to hunt for Kate or even try to clear his own name. He'd been jailed with bail set so high he could never make it—not even if every friend he had chipped in. The only way he was going to get out of the cell he was in would be a transfer to the state prison in Huntsville. He flopped back on his bed in defeat.

In a moment he sat up. Instead of moping around, he needed to call his lawyer and arrange for the sale of his home—that was the only way he'd generate enough funds to make bail. Thank goodness Bradley Alain, the topmost criminal lawyer in east Texas, had volunteered to defend him. Otherwise he'd have to sell his house for legal fees alone.

If Molly Harper had done nothing else, she'd inspired him to quit wallowing around and imagining the awfulness of Anna's last moments and do something to help himself. She'd walked into the jail and brought his hopes back to life. "Damn," he muttered.

The man in the cell next to him spoke. "Hey, Lakeman, I hear you're going to get the chair."

"Shut up," Thomas said.

"My lawyer tells me that Texas executes more people than any other state."

"Shut up!" Thomas grasped the bars as if he intended to pull them apart. "Just shut up!" But now he was speaking to himself, to the part of him that, once again, had begun to imagine Anna's last moments.

IT WAS MIDDAY, the February sun warm as Molly stepped out of the Jeep in the midst of huge trees and the chirping of birds. Spring was still several weeks away, but the forest was waking up from the sleep of winter.

Familiar hopped out of the vehicle and started immediately to the abandoned tent that remained at the campsite where Thomas had spent Saturday night. Molly approached slowly, taking in the evidence that told of a hurried departure.

There were the cold embers of a fire and a camp coffeepot sitting beside it. She touched the pot with her toe. Coffee sloshed in it. About ten yards away, Familiar was entering the tent.

Beside the fire she found a Coleman lantern and a tin cup. Closer to the tent was a flashlight lying on a bed of pine needles and beside that a battered ice chest. The police hadn't bothered to pick up any of Thomas's gear. She lifted the lid of the chest and found three unopened beers, water, coffee, some apples and bologna. It certainly looked as if Thomas had been camping in earnest.

So far, everything he'd said had checked out, but if he'd set up the campsite as an alibi, of course it would. She was reluctant to enter the tent, and that emotion surprised her. For some reason she felt as if she were invading Thomas's privacy. Even though he'd requested as much.

"Familiar!" She went to the tent flap. The cat had found plenty to explore. He'd been inside the tent for more than fifteen minutes. "Kitty, kitty."

The cat sauntered outside with what looked to be part of a newspaper. She knelt to take it and the cat used his paw to point out the date. February 17. It was the Saturday evening that Anna had been killed.

"This doesn't prove anything." She folded the paper and put it in her pocket. "Thomas Lakeman could have planted that newspaper. He could have bought it and left it just to attempt to show he was here." The newspaper didn't prove a thing, but it was good to have.

The cat gave one cry and began to walk the area. Molly watched him in awe as he created a spiral and worked his way from the inside out, examining the ground, sniffing the grass. She'd never seen a detective, much less a cat, conduct such an intense investigation.

When he paused about twenty yards away, she went to see what he'd found. "A clue?"

Familiar pointed to a hole in the ground. "Snake?" she asked, remembering that her father had always told her that snakes lived in holes. Though she enjoyed the woods, she was wary of the wild creatures, particularly snakes. The motto in Texas was that everything was bigger, and that certainly applied to the rattlers. A timber rattler could grow up to six feet long and as big around as a man's muscular arm.

The cat left his find and walked to another place. He stared at her until she followed him. Another hole. She frowned, realizing the cat was showing her a pattern.

There were four holes on each side of the square and two larger ones in between. She understood. "A tent. So Thomas wasn't lying about that. Someone else was camping here." Why was the cat trying so hard to convince her of Thomas's innocence? The answer was obvious—because he believed Thomas wasn't guilty.

"Why would someone kill my sister, steal her baby and set Thomas Lakeman up to take the fall? Why him? If he's telling the truth, he was just my sister's friend."

The cat didn't have an answer, or if he did he wasn't saying. But the question throbbed in Molly's brain. Ever since she'd heard the awful news, she'd asked herself who would hurt her sweet sister. The name that always came up was Darwin Goodman. She didn't say it, but in her opinion he was awful enough to sell his own child. And if a lot of money were involved, he'd even kill.

"We have to get back to the jail," she said. "I have another question for Thomas."

*My PRELIMINARY INVESTIGATION supports everything Thomas said at the jail. There is a second campsite where two people slept. And whoever they were, they left in a big hurry. At night. I found some of their gear scattered at the edge of the clearing, which leads me to believe they left before first light. That makes me wonder if they had a reason to be gone. Sure, I have a suspicious mind, but that's why*

*I'm such a good detective. I don't let a motive sneak up on me—I like to see it coming.*

*Call me a trained observer, but I detect a bit of chemistry between Molly and Thomas. She doesn't trust him, not by a long shot, but she felt something for him. If she hadn't, she'd never have gone to check out his campsite. One thing I've learned as a private dick is to always suspect the worst of human nature. Thomas, though, strikes me as a good man. Molly asked the right question—if Thomas is innocent, why was he set up? I think that's how we're going to have to approach this. Thomas is the key.*

*With that in mind, I hope Miss Molly Marvel doesn't blow a gasket when she realizes what I have planned.*

*We're back at the county lockup. It isn't the most sophisticated jail I've ever seen. In fact, it's pretty minimum security. They're treating Thomas like he's some kind of hardcore felon, but I suspect they leave him pretty much to himself once he's back in his cell.*

*It's a simple lock and key system and I didn't notice any security monitors. Should be a piece of cake. I just hope Molly can handle it.*

"MR. LAKEMAN, why would someone frame you?" Molly asked him.

Thomas found himself sitting in the interview room yet again, with the beautiful brunette seated across from him. A week ago he would have been planning a way to ask her for a date. Now he was hoping not to frighten her so badly she wouldn't listen to what he had to say.

"I think I was convenient. Anna always turned to me when she was in trouble. There were a few times when she spent the night at my house with Kate. Darwin was drunk and she didn't want to go home."

He could see what she was thinking and he shook his head. "Nothing like that happened. Anna and I were friends. Nothing more. You don't know me at all, but you should know your sister took her marriage vows seriously."

"And how do you know that?" Molly's question sounded angry.

"She could have left Darwin and started a new life, but she wouldn't. She never gave up on her marriage. She was committed to it." He watched her expression change. Something he'd said wounded her, but he couldn't figure out what.

"It's too bad she couldn't commit to a man who didn't slap her around." Molly's voice was hard.

Thomas swallowed and looked down at his hands. He knew for a fact that Darwin had beaten—not just slapped—Anna. But it would only hurt Molly to think of her sister's abuse. Better to keep the ugly details to himself.

"So you believe you were just a convenient scapegoat?" Molly asked him.

"What else can I believe? I don't have a lot of money. I write software for computers. That isn't the most controversial career." He saw her look at his hands, the rough callused palms. His face, too, had seen sun and weather. Even though he'd been working indoors for the past two years, he knew he still carried the look of the open range in his features. "Before I got this job I worked as a cowboy on one of the large spreads." That was as much as he intended to tell her.

"That's a jump in career choices."

He thought he detected amusement in her tone, and it burned him. "If I've answered all your questions, I'd like to go back to my cell."

When he stood, the guard was instantly at his side, almost as if he feared Thomas might get a second victim. "I'm done here," Thomas said, and walked to the door so he wouldn't have to see the guard and Molly exchange glances.

"Mr. Lakeman, I'm not finished."

"Lakeman!" The guard stepped in front of him.

Thomas turned back to face Molly, a dare in his eyes. If he hadn't realized before how much of his rights had been taken, he knew now. He didn't even have the right to terminate a conversation with a condescending woman. They might make him stay in the room, but he wasn't going to talk.

To his surprise he saw Molly look down at the table. She understood what had been taken from him. "Guard, Mr. Lakeman doesn't have to talk to me." She stood up. "Thank you for your time, Mr. Lakeman."

MOLLY STOOD in the reception area of the lockup waiting for Familiar. The cat had disappeared the moment she entered the building. Now there was no trace of him. She tried not to appear impatient. What would she answer if someone asked who she was waiting for?

She sat on one of the hard benches set against the wall and tried to gather her thoughts. The bottom line was that she was no closer to finding baby Kate than she had been five hours before. The clock was ticking away and she was useless.

She waited twenty minutes before she stood and walked to the door that led to the cells. It was shut, and above it in large black letters were the words: Authorized Personnel Only. She opened it a crack to see if she could catch a glimpse of Familiar. He'd darted to the left, toward the cells, when the guard had taken her to the interview room on the right.

She thought an alarm might sound when she opened the door, but to her surprise nothing happened. It was going on five o'clock, and the few office workers were preparing to leave. No one seemed particularly interested in what she was doing.

But where was that darn cat?

The door was painfully wrenched out of her hand and she was pushed back into the waiting room by a large man.

"What—"

"Give me your keys!"

At first she didn't recognize Thomas Lakeman, but when she did, she froze. He was out of his handcuffs and out of his cell.

"Molly, give me your keys!" He increased his grip on her arm enough to startle her out of her shock.

"What's going on?"

Before Thomas could answer, Familiar appeared from around the corner, jumped onto her purse, and tugged it from her arm. In a flash he'd dug out her car keys and scooted them across the floor to Thomas.

Without ever letting go of her arm, Thomas scooped up the purse, the keys and the cat. Dragging her behind him he ran out the front door of the building.

"I'm sorry," he said as he pushed her into the passenger seat of her car. In five seconds he was behind the wheel with Familiar right behind him.

Thomas burned rubber as he put the eight-cylinder SUV in reverse and pulled out in front of oncoming traffic. Without a second's hesitation, he jammed the gas pedal to the floor and the car shot forward as several police officers swarmed out of the building.

"Stop!" an officer cried as he drew his weapon.

Molly felt Thomas's hand on her neck as he pressed her down. The passenger window exploded and then they were gone. Behind them several panicked drivers had collided, effectively blocking the street.

Molly sat up. She didn't really believe what had happened. Thomas had escaped from jail. In her vehicle. With her as a hostage. She felt as if adrenaline had been mainlined into her heart.

"It's going to be okay," Thomas said, his gaze on the road.

"Are you insane?" she asked.

"Technically, no." Thomas glanced at her for a second, then turned his gaze back to the road. "I'm not insane, but I am desperate. I just wanted to thank you."

"*Thank* me?" She couldn't believe this. She was his hostage and he was thanking her. She'd almost been hit by a police bullet because of him, and he was thanking her. He *was* insane.

"I still don't know how you trained that cat, but I have to hand it to you. I've never seen anything like it."

Molly had a sick feeling. Familiar sat between them, his attention totally on the road. She remembered the way he'd pawed the map, insisting that she go to the state park to check out Thomas's story. The way he'd shown her the tent stake holes. What had he done?

"Any fool knows you can't train a cat." She glared at Familiar.

"Somebody trained this one, and whoever it was did one hell of a job."

"What did Familiar do?" She'd fire him on the spot. She'd buy a cat carrier, stuff him in it and put him on the first plane back to Washington, D.C.

"He was in my cell when I came back from the interview room. I'd seen him around earlier, but I didn't realize he was your cat until he started to act strange."

One thing about Familiar—he could certainly act strange when he chose to. "Go on," she said.

"He walked right out of my cell and went down to where the guard sits. I was watching, just amazed. The cat reached up and snagged the cell key. That quick." Thomas snapped his fingers. "Then he brought it to me. Thank goodness they haven't modernized the jail or it would be a different story. As it was, it was just like one of those Wild West shows. I unlocked the cell and walked right out."

Molly knew better. "It was just that easy until what?"

"Until I had to knock the deputy out."

"Good grief," she muttered. "You struck a deputy?"

"He was about to yell and alert the others. I didn't have a choice."

She wanted to punch him. "Of course you had a choice. You could have stayed in the cell."

"Now why would I do that when you went to all that trouble to spring me?"

Thomas took a hard right and headed up into what looked to be high hills or small mountains.

"Where are we going?" For a moment Molly was distracted from her plight by a bigger worry. What did Thomas intend to do with her?

"These are the foothills of the Ozark Mountains. I know some good places to hide out."

She sighed. "We need to get a couple of things straight right now. I didn't train the cat to help you escape." She picked Familiar up and held him so she could stare into his green eyes. "That was his idea all by himself."

Thomas laughed. "Try telling that to the deputies. I'm sure they'll get a big laugh as they lock you up."

"It's the truth." She put Familiar down on the seat, suddenly feeling how deep her troubles were. She'd been involved in a felony jailbreak. It didn't matter that she was an innocent victim. It was her vehicle that had been used for the getaway. No one would ever believe she was innocent.

"The truth doesn't matter, Miss Harper."

"I didn't plan this or help you. I'm innocent."

He slowed long enough to look directly into her eyes. "Welcome to my world."

## *Chapter Three*

Thomas knew he'd shocked Molly, but she had to understand the score or she'd get hurt. No matter what her intentions—and if she hadn't put the cat up to springing him, who had?—she was now involved. He might regret that she'd been dragged into the mess, but he certainly didn't regret having his freedom. If he was going to prove his innocence, he had to be free to do it. Certainly no one wearing a badge seemed interested in seeking the evidence that would counter the circumstantial case against him.

"Miss Harper, I'm not going to hurt you, but I may need to keep your vehicle."

Molly stared out the front window as if she'd gone into some kind of trance. Worry etched fine lines around her eyes, and Thomas felt a pang. This woman had lost her sister and her niece. Now, because of him, she was in trouble with the law.

"I'm sorry." He meant it. "When I can, I'll let you loose. I'll call the sheriff's office and tell them you weren't involved in the breakout."

"And they'll believe you."

The heavy dose of sarcasm in her tone actually made Thomas feel better. She was a fighter. "Why did you send the cat in to get the key if you didn't want me to escape?"

The look she shot him would curdle milk. He automatically pressed harder on the gas pedal.

She raised her chin defiantly. "I didn't send the cat. He went on his own."

"You'd better come up with something more reasonable than that if you want the deputies to believe you." It was sort of ironic. They were both at a place where their stories were "too convenient." "Look at it from my perspective. You show up out of the blue and insist on talking to me. You come back twice in one day. And the second time, while we're talking, the cat is casing the joint to plot an escape. Doesn't that seem like you might have planned it? Heck, even the idea that a cat obeys your command is hard to believe. But that the cat *planned* it? Get a grip."

He could see she understood, even if it was against her will. It was easier for her to be angry at him than it was to think how her own actions had put her in jeopardy.

"I didn't plan a thing except for a talk with you." She nudged the cat. "That's what I get for listening to him. He insisted we go to the campsite. He found the place where those other campers pitched a tent. He's your biggest supporter and fan."

Thomas chuckled. He couldn't help it. In another time and place he'd think about calling the men with the white coats for a woman who spoke about a cat as if he were human.

She slumped deeper into her seat. "You're laughing at me like I'm a nut."

He wisely kept his mouth shut and focused on the road. The sun had set behind the hills, and the blue-gray of twilight had turned the trees into stark black silhouettes. It was the most beautiful and the saddest time of day to him.

"Familiar is a private investigator." She spoke softly, as if she didn't believe the words. "I hired him yesterday and picked him up at the airport in Shreveport, Louisiana, this morning."

He chanced a look. She'd really blown a

fuse—she thought the cat was a detective. "You picked him up? Like at the baggage claim?"

"He flew in from D.C. First class. I hired Familiar to find Kate. He's got a résumé that includes solving murders, kidnappings and busting international crime rings. All he's done here is involve me in a jailbreak with the man charged with my sister's murder." Now it was her turn to laugh.

As Molly grew quiet, Thomas turned on the SUV's lights. They cut a broad path through the gathering darkness, and to his left he saw a herd of white-tailed deer grazing. The light was poor, but he thought they were all does, the females who'd managed to survive the most recent season of hunting.

Thomas failed to see the sport in it when the hunter had a high-powered rifle, scopes that practically sighted the gun, a four-wheeler to cover ground, and walkie-talkies to conspire with his buddies. There wasn't much sport in killing an animal whose only defense was flight.

"You look like you could spit nails," she commented. "What's wrong with you?"

"I was thinking about hunters."

She shook her head. "I don't want to try to

understand how your mind works." She sat up taller. "Where are you taking me?"

"I have a friend who has a cabin. It's a bit primitive, but you'll be warm and safe."

"Can't you just let us out of the car? We're a thousand miles from nowhere. I haven't seen another car for the last hour. If you let Familiar and me out, it'll take us two days to walk back to civilization."

He considered it. "No."

"Why not? You say you don't intend to hurt us."

"Something bad could happen to you."

She raised her hands in disgust. "Something other than being taken hostage by an escaped murderer?"

"I'm not a murderer. I'm falsely charged. And I don't consider this a dangerous situation because I won't hurt you."

"I'm supposed to take your word for that."

"Look." He was getting annoyed. "You don't have any choice but to take my word. There are wild animals in these woods. Normally they avoid humans, but it would be my luck that I would put you out and a mountain lion would eat you. Now let me drive. It's dark. The road has gotten narrow. I haven't been back here in the past five years, and I don't want to get lost. We have only a quarter tank of gas."

Those words silenced her, and Thomas's thoughts turned to the real danger of their situation. If they ran out of gas up in this area, they might wait around for days before anyone happened along. February wasn't a big camping month and though the weather was mild now, a blizzard could pass through and they could easily freeze to death.

They wound higher into the hills, and Thomas had the sense that they'd entered a tunnel of trees. No stars were visible through the thick canopy of limbs. During the day it was beautiful. At night it felt a bit claustrophobic.

"Have you thought far enough ahead to figure out what you're going to do?" she asked. "You're free, but you don't have a life. You can't go back to your home. You can't go to your job. What are you going to do?"

He didn't have a specific plan, but he had an answer. "I'm going to prove my innocence. And I'm going to find Kate, if she's alive. I've been sitting in that jail cell since Anna was killed. I haven't had a chance to look for Kate. Now I will."

Her voice was softer. "Do you believe she's alive?"

As much as he wanted to lie to her, he had to tell the truth. "I don't know. I want to believe she's okay, but the sheriff has everyone convinced that she's dead. He must have found something at the scene to make him so sure."

"Has anyone talked to Darwin?" she asked.

He shook his head. "He wouldn't talk to me. We had a heated set-to at my arraignment. I accused him of killing Anna and he screamed at me and accused me of killing his wife and baby. It was high drama on his part."

"He was acting?"

"Darwin hardly knows me, but I think he knows I didn't hurt Anna or Kate. We had words a few months ago after he'd hit Anna and she came to my house. He wanted to say we were having an affair, but I straightened him out." His hands tightened on the wheel as he remembered. "I wanted to punch his lights out, but I couldn't. I might've had a moment's satisfaction, but Anna would have lost the only safe place she had to go."

"You said high drama. Why would he accuse you of killing her?"

"He didn't want the cops looking at him.

I was the perfect scapegoat, and he played it to the hilt. How well do you know him?"

"The first time I met him was at the wedding." Molly cleared her throat. "He was crude and awful. I guess I wanted my sister to have that fairy-tale love story—the prince on a white horse who would rescue her and love her and take care of her. Darwin was about as far from that as anyone can get. He married Anna for her inheritance. And when he went through all of her money, he started hitting her."

"He's a real charmer."

"How often did you see Anna? Thomas, you have to tell me the truth. I have to know the facts if I'm going to figure out what happened to Katie."

Thomas knew she was asking how often her sister received a beating at the hands of her husband. Earlier he'd tried to protect her from the truth about her sister's abuse, but now he felt he had to tell her. "Anna came by sporadically, either when she was really happy or really scared."

The dash light of the SUV gave Molly's face a soft illumination, and he saw the tear trace down her cheek. She was hearing some hard things, but if she wanted to find Katie, she would have to hear a lot more.

He kept his gaze on the road as he talked. "About once a week Anna would come over because she was afraid. Either he'd already hit her or he'd threatened to hit her."

"When she was pregnant..."

"Toward the end he just slapped her. He had some restraint. He never took it far enough to break a bone or do any permanent damage. It was more about bullying Anna, about breaking her down. The emotional pain was far worse than the physical."

Now Molly's tears flowed in earnest. He slowed the vehicle, but she waved him on. "I'm okay," she said. "I just wish she'd called me. I suspected she was unhappy, but whenever I spoke to her, she said she was happy and for me to mind my own business."

"It was so important to her for you to believe she was a success. That she'd made the right choice." Thomas thought about the conversations he'd had with Anna. "She felt like a failure. She was the college dropout, the one who couldn't get it right. She knew she'd worried your mom a lot. After your mother died, she felt like she had to prove to you that she was smart and strong and able to manage her own life."

"You see how well that went."

"There was nothing you could have done. Honestly. I tried. I begged her to leave Darwin, to take Kate and start over fresh. I offered her money, contacts, whatever she needed. She wouldn't go."

"She was hardheaded like that."

"Anna looked up to you. She talked all the time about her sister, Molly, about how talented you were and how you were living in Arizona on an Indian reservation and helping the tribes market their jewelry and crafts." She wasn't crying any longer, but in the quick glance he shot her, he could see the pain on her face. Thomas wanted to ease her suffering. He knew enough about loss to know that a few well-placed words could last a lifetime. "Anna admired you so much. She said you'd gotten all the strength in the family. That you didn't need a husband or anyone. She thought that was great."

Molly sighed. "That's funny because she told me I was too ornery to catch a man."

It was the first time he'd seen her really smile, and it literally made him catch his breath. There was something in Molly Harper's smile that touched his heart and made a shiver rush through him.

"You okay?" she asked.

He nodded. "I guess someone just walked over my grave."

IN THE BLACKNESS of the wilderness, Molly didn't see the outline of the cabin until the SUV's lights struck the cypress exterior. She suppressed a shudder. The cabin was dark and lonely looking, but she needed to get out of the vehicle. She felt as if she'd been riding in darkness for half her life.

"Let me go in first and check it out." Thomas got out of the SUV, pocketing the keys and her only chance of escape.

In truth, even if she had had the keys, she would have had no idea how to get out of the forest. The road had switched back and forth. Thomas had taken turnoffs that seemed to repeat themselves every ten miles. With less than a quarter tank of gas, she might end up hopelessly lost.

Familiar, her legendary private investigator, had napped most of the way. She nudged the cat. "Wake up."

Familiar stood, arched his back and yawned. He certainly wasn't concerned about their plight. He hopped from the vehicle and trotted behind Thomas up the steps of the

cabin. The two of them disappeared from the light cast by the vehicle's headlamps.

Molly got out and stretched. The woods were alive with sound. Insects, the rustle of leaves and branches that could be deer—or something more sinister. She hurried after Thomas. It was his bright idea to bring her there, and if someone was going to be eaten by a wild animal, it was going to be him.

Inside the cabin a lantern flared to life. The warm glow revealed a comfortable front room. Rocking chairs were drawn before a cold fireplace. There was a stout wooden table and cast-iron cooking utensils hanging on the wall behind it. A thin coating of dust covered everything, but otherwise the cabin was carefully maintained.

"I'll get some wood." Thomas acted on his words. Molly took the lamp and examined the rest of the house. There was a kitchen and a single bedroom. Her anger flared.

Thomas entered with an armload of wood. As he bent to light the fire, she rounded on him. "If you think you can hold me here, you've got another think coming. I have to get on with my search for Katie."

Ignoring her, Thomas struck a match and

the dry wood gave a cheerful crackle. He rose slowly and looked at her.

"You can't leave tonight." He looked at the fire. "You can have the bed. I'll sleep on the floor here by the fire. I'm going to check for supplies in the kitchen. There probably won't be much, but we might be able to find some beans or something."

With that he was gone. Molly stood, hands on her hips, frustration gnawing at her gut. She wasn't a single step closer to finding her niece.

She pulled the note from her pocket and read it again. The words seemed more ominous.

"The baby is alive. Don't stop hunting, but don't go to the police."

"What's that you're reading?"

She lowered the note and turned to find Thomas standing not five feet away, his gaze on the scrap of paper.

"It's why I'm here." She handed it to him and watched his face as he read it.

"Is this for real?"

"I don't know." She bit her bottom lip. "I have to believe it's real. I have to hang on to the idea that Katie's alive. That's why I have to get out of here now."

He nodded. "You received this in Arizona? At your home?"

"Yes. Day before yesterday."

"Via the mail? Where's the envelope?"

"It was mailed from here in Jefferson."

Thomas's face actually showed hope. "So the person who mailed it knows your physical address and knows your relationship to Katie. That's good, I think."

"Are they going to demand a ransom?" Molly asked.

Thomas threw more wood on the fire and held his hands out to it. "I don't know. That note doesn't have the sound of someone seeking a ransom. In fact, it sounds more like someone trying to tip you off. Is there someone at your home checking the mail, in case they contact you again?"

"I have a friend I can call to do that."

"Good. But you should warn your friend that the police may be watching him."

If Molly hadn't realized how serious her situation was, Thomas's words brought it home. "Why would they be watching my friends?" Reality touched her. "Because they think I'm on the lam with an escaped murderer." It was a statement.

Thomas nodded. "Either as a hostage or a co-conspirator in a jail escape, you're going to be of interest to law enforcement. And so

will your friends or anyone seen going in
and out of your home."

"But that could work to our advantage,
couldn't it?" She felt a surge of hope. "The
police haven't shown a lot of interest in
searching for Kate, but if they're looking for
me, they might find the baby."

Thomas smiled. He couldn't help it. Molly
Harper had spunk. "That's one way to turn it
to a positive light."

"What's the point of being negative?" She
paced the cabin. "But we do have to resolve
this—" she waved her hand around the room
"—hostage thing."

"What do you suggest?" Thomas asked.

She could see he was willing to listen. In-
itially she'd been mad at him, but now she
felt the anger slipping away. He was only
trying to get his life back. She'd lost her sister
and her niece, but he'd lost big, too. He'd lost
his identity and, if he was telling the truth,
only because he'd been kind to Anna.

"We can play it two ways. I can turn
myself in and say you released me, or we
can team up and try to outrun the law."

He was very still, but his gaze never left
hers. "You'd risk it all by teaming up with me?
You believe me when I say I'm innocent?"

She swallowed. "Right this moment, I believe you. Please don't give me any reason not to."

She felt the sharp claws of the cat digging into her shin. Leaning down, she pulled him into her arms. "You haven't been a lot of help, Familiar."

"Meow!" He struggled in her arms and she released him. In a moment he was patting her pocket where she'd put the note. She pulled it out and spread it on top of the table where the cat sat in front of it as if he were reading.

"Meow," he said, putting his paw on the words *The baby is alive.*

Molly inhaled sharply. "The person who wrote this note knows enough about my family to track me down. This had to be someone that Anna talked to."

"And that's the best clue yet," Thomas said, nodding.

## Chapter Four

Molly watched Thomas's skill with the open fireplace and the food he'd prepared. He'd taken basic canned goods and come up with a meal, including hot coffee. "I guess you really enjoy camping," she said. She didn't add that her idea of a weekend off included a massage and room service.

"It was part of a life I left behind." He unhooked the pot from the cast-iron brace and carried it to the table. "If I had my druthers, I'd still be out on the range."

"You're a computer software designer, right?" Molly found the two careers—software designer and cowboy—almost diametrically opposed.

"That's right. I work in the Security Department at McGivens. We write programs to protect computer networks from privacy threats."

She laughed. "I don't see what that has to do with herding cows."

Thomas signaled for her to have a seat. He served them both some beans and corn bread before he sat down across from her. Familiar nibbled daintily on the corned beef Thomas had opened for him.

"Nothing to do with the cows, but with the strategy for keeping the cows safe," he explained. "It isn't the same, but sometimes it requires the same mindset—to see danger on the horizon and figure a way to head it off at the pass."

He was entertaining her, trying to keep her mind off the crazy twist her life had taken, and she appreciated his efforts. "So why did you leave the open range?"

"The big cattle companies are breaking up the family ranches. The new breed of rancher sits in an office in Houston and wants to feed-lot the cows. It's not a business I want to be involved in anymore. I had a buddy in computer security. Turns out I had an aptitude for it. I got training and a job."

She could understand that. Once, a cowboy rode miles and miles of open land pushing cattle from pasture to pasture. It was a job description that fit the cowboy's need for wide-open space, self-reliance and a bond with nature. Now it was a business where a cow was born and died within the same small compound.

Thomas shook his head, and a sheepish grin touched his features. "I'd be laughed off the ranch, but I'm a vegetarian these days."

The light from the fire danced across his features, and Molly thought, not for the first time, what an attractive man he was. His brown hair was cut short and neat, and his hazel eyes glittered with intelligence tempered by kindness. His build bespoke of long days with little attention paid to food, yet he was an excellent cook. He was a man filled with complexities. She looked down at her plate of beans. "I don't miss the meat, but a glass of wine would be nice," she said.

He frowned. "We're going to need supplies. I'm sure my bank account is being watched, which means I can't withdraw funds."

"I have some cash." She surprised herself. She was offering aid to the man who'd abducted her. "And a credit card, but they're probably watching my accounts, too."

He pushed his half-eaten food back. "I've

been thinking, Molly. You should call the police. Tell them you were abducted and that I let you go. You can go on with your search for Kate without being involved in my troubles."

Across the table, Familiar stopped eating and looked at her.

Molly was shocked—at her reaction. Thomas was offering her freedom, and she found herself resisting the idea. Had she lost her mind? "What if the police think I was involved in breaking you out of jail? They'll just arrest me, and I'll be behind bars and unable to hunt for Kate."

"I suspect they'll assume you were innocently taken by the mad killer of your sister." Thomas didn't bother to hide the bitter hurt in his voice. "If you tell them I took you by force, they'll believe you. They'll want to believe you because it fits in with their idea that I killed my friend and did something awful to her baby."

"They might not believe me. I don't want to risk it." Molly had a mental image of a thermometer shooting up to 105 degrees. Her brain was really cooking! She was trying to convince her abductor to let her stay. What was it called? The Stockholm Syndrome, when a captive began to identify with her abductor?

"We need to hear the news," Thomas said. "That way we can get a line on what the law is thinking." He looked around the cabin.

"There's no electricity, much less television," Molly pointed out.

"Meow!" Familiar reached across the table and snagged the sleeve of Thomas's shirt. "Meow."

The cat hopped down and walked to the door. He cast a solemn green gaze on Thomas and Molly and waited at the door.

"He wants us to follow him," Molly said, rising.

"How can you tell?" Thomas didn't move.

"Trust me, we should follow him or else he'll come over and bite your shins."

Thomas rose. "So we'll follow him."

Molly caught the tone of condescension in his voice, and she smiled. Familiar would make a believer of him—and soon.

They stepped into the night, following the cat in the beam of lantern light that fell from the open door. Familiar sauntered to the SUV where he stood on his back legs and patted the door of the vehicle.

Molly opened the door and he hopped in, his black paw batting the radio.

"He's right," Thomas said. "I can't believe he thought of it before we did." His voice held awe. "The radio could have a story on us."

"I told you the cat was a detective," Molly said, sliding into the driver's seat. "Give me the keys."

Thomas handed them over and she turned on the ignition. After spinning the dial, she finally found a crackly newscast.

Through the static, the newscaster's voice sounded serious. "Law enforcement officials in a five-county area are searching for an escapee tonight. Sheriff Paul Johnson has issued an alert to the area citizenry to be on the lookout for Thomas Lakeman. The thirty-eight-year-old man is accused of murder in the shooting death of thirty-year-old Anna Goodman. It is believed the victim's sister, Molly Harper, has been taken hostage by the accused murderer. Miss Harper was at the jail earlier today when Lakeman made his escape. Missing in the case and presumed dead is the nine-month-old daughter of the slain victim. We'll have an update on this story on the hour."

Molly snapped the radio off. She had to admit that Thomas was right. The best course of action would be to go back and tell the police she'd been abducted. That way she'd be able to access funds and help Thomas.

"You see why you should go back to Jefferson?" he asked.

She nodded and looked at him standing in the doorway of the vehicle. "I don't think you killed my sister."

Relief swept across his features. "Do you mean that?"

"Yes. I'll go back to town and get some money and ask some questions, then I'll meet you. We'll figure a way to get a car for you."

"I can't believe you're going to help me."

"It's not just about you. The person who killed Anna is still out there, and my niece is missing. If we find the real killer, he'll be able to tell us where Kate is."

Thomas put his hand on her arm. Molly felt a warm flush move through her body as she stared into his hazel eyes. How long had it been since she'd been moved by a touch? She didn't even want to think about it.

"I'm going to make you a promise, Molly Harper," Thomas said, his voice soft but steely. "We're going to find Kate and bring her home to you. No matter what we have to do to find her."

"Meow!" Familiar jumped into Molly's lap and put his paw on top of Thomas's hand.

KNEELING IN FRONT of the fireplace, Thomas added another log to the fire. He felt Molly's gaze on him and wondered what she was thinking.

Sparks flew up the chimney from the new log, and he thought how fleeting so many things in life were. Only a week ago Anna Goodman had sat on his leather sofa holding little Kate in her lap. Anna had been crying, but she hadn't been hurt. Deep in her eyes had been resolve to leave Darwin and build a new life. If he thought about it hard enough, he could hear her voice, the unexpected strength she'd found. And he could so clearly remember his pride in her, and his relief that she was finally going to do something to protect herself and her baby.

Now she was dead.

When the sheriff's deputies had shaken him awake in his sleeping bag, he'd been puzzled but unconcerned.

"What's going on?" he'd asked as he'd gotten out of the bag and reached for the coffee to brew a fresh pot. The deputy had snapped the cuffs on his wrist and read him his rights. They'd searched through his things looking for evidence of some crime they wouldn't even define for him. When they'd found nothing they'd shoved him into a car and driven him to the station.

The entire ride Thomas had been confused, but under the assumption that he could clear matters up. There had surely been a mistake.

When he'd heard that Anna had been murdered—shot in his home—he'd been too stunned to think clearly. In the eyes of the investigating deputy, Thomas had looked guilty.

The arraignment and grand jury indictment had followed swiftly. The small town of Jefferson didn't see a lot of murders. The wheels of justice were set in motion almost before he could find a lawyer to defend him. Bradley Alain had put a halt on the railroad job that was in progress, but Thomas was still charged with a crime he didn't commit.

"Thomas, are you okay?"

Molly's question brought him back to the present, and he felt an unexpected rush of pleasure as he rose and turned to face her. The firelight flickered over her classic features, catching in the lengths of her hair. The black cat lay across her lap, enjoying the strokes she applied so liberally.

"I was just trying to figure out how all of this happened. Most of my life has been calm and orderly. Get up at five, eat breakfast, saddle my horse and ride out. Come home at supper, eat, wash up, play some cards with the guys or go into town. At McGivens, it was work eight hours, go home. Same thing, day in and day out."

"Now it's much different."

"That's an understatement. I'm a fugitive from the law, accused of a crime I didn't commit. I have a hostage and her black cat detective." He shook his head. "Have we stumbled into the Twilight Zone?"

"I feel the same way."

A wistful look crossed her face, and Thomas felt a pang. As awful as his life was at the moment, he hadn't lost family. "We'll find Kate," he said again.

Molly smiled. "We will." She stopped petting the cat.

"It won't bring Anna back, I know. But she'd finally decided to leave Darwin. She was getting stronger. I think Kate was the best thing that ever happened to her."

Molly looked up, unshed tears shimmering in her eyes. "Anna was always in hot water somewhere. In high school she was constantly in trouble. When she got out, she didn't want to go to college, but she couldn't hold a job. When she finally went to university, every week it was a crisis with one class or another." She bit her bottom lip. "I got tired of her woes, tired of trying to bail her out so she could make the same mistake again and again. I abandoned her."

Thomas sat beside her. In his adult solitary life, he'd been careful never to assume emotional responsibility for anyone other than himself. But he understood guilt, and he knew that was what Molly felt. Survivor's guilt.

"Molly, you and I both know that no one can force another person to confront their problems and grow up. If you'd continued to hold Anna's hand, she may never have begun to change."

"If I'd held her hand a little more, she might be alive to change."

He picked up her hand, noting the long, slender fingers. "I'm just a software designer, so I don't have any deep answers. I will tell you what Anna said the last time I saw her." The night she was killed. He didn't say it, but they both knew it.

"Tell me she was happy." Molly blinked back the tears.

"I can, without lying." Thomas squeezed her cool fingers. "When Anna showed up with Kate, I was worried. I was afraid Darwin was thumping on her again, but he wasn't. In fact, Anna had come to visit because she had good news. She said she was leaving the software company, that she'd found a better job, one where she could work at home and stay with Kate more." He could see he'd caught Molly's interest.

"What kind of job?"

"She said it was a secret until it was a done deal. With the new salary, she said she could afford to divorce Darwin and still take care of Kate."

"She stood up to him? Do you think that made him kill her?"

Thomas hesitated. "From what I knew of Darwin, material things were very important to him. At first I was worried, too, but Anna said she'd told him she didn't want anything. No furniture, no alimony. She just said she'd leave with nothing."

"That was smart, but it's hard to believe Darwin was agreeable to this."

Thomas still held Molly's hand. It had grown warmer in his grasp, and he rubbed the top of it with his thumb. "Anna said that

Darwin was surprised, but he was rational. She told me she'd been thinking, and she'd decided that she could relocate. She was the happiest I'd ever seen her, like she'd just gotten the best news in the world."

Molly nodded. "Anna could have done anything she wanted to do. She just never believed in herself."

Thomas leaned closer. "She said you always believed in her and encouraged her, and now she was going to prove that you were right. She was going to change her life."

Molly choked back a sob. "I would have helped her. I would have done anything for her and Kate."

"She knew that, but she also knew she needed to do it on her own. She saw a completely different life ahead of her, and she was ready to make it happen. She found her belief in herself."

"And then she died." Molly's face settled into an angry expression. "She was murdered."

Thomas released her hand. "It's true. But I think it's important for you to know that Anna was on the road to change. She adored you, Molly. You were her hero. And before she died, she felt she could be your equal. That's an important thing to hang on to. All of the love and effort you gave Anna paid off."

Molly got up and went to the fireplace. She used the poker to stir the logs, sending a shower of sparks up the chimney. "I have so many regrets."

Thomas hesitated, then went to her side. He put an arm around her. Her shoulders were slender, and he could feel the pent-up tension in her. "If Anna were alive now, would she want you to blame yourself?"

Molly smiled. "Anna didn't like blame."

"She was right about that part. Blame doesn't do anyone any good. She talked about your work with the American Indians and the good things you were accomplishing. You were doing what you were meant to do. Anna would only have resented any effort you made in trying to straighten up her life."

Molly looked up at him. He could see the sadness in her gaze, but there was also a spark of humor. "You really were her friend, weren't you?"

"Yes. We were friends."

"It gives me comfort to know that. She had you to turn to." Molly stepped closer and brushed a kiss across his cheek.

The kiss was one of gratitude, but Thomas

felt it to the bottom of his boots. Molly Harper was a dangerous woman. "You should get some rest," he said. "Tomorrow is going to be a taxing day."

She lingered next to him for a moment, as if she were drawing from his strength. When she stepped away, she called the cat to follow her into the bedroom. The door closed, and Thomas settled onto the sofa, wondering if the tumultuous rush of his thoughts would allow him any rest.

*AT LEAST THE COWBOY and Molly have come to an agreement. I was getting a little concerned at first. They need each other to find baby Kate, and to bring the murderer to justice.*

*I took one look at Thomas and knew he hadn't killed anyone. He's a rough-and-tumble guy, a cowboy, but there's a gentleness about him that marks him as one of the good guys. Maybe when we go into town tomorrow I should buy him a white hat. Make him a little more easily identifiable. But I doubt we'll have time for a shopping spree. Too much to do.*

*The person who killed Anna is very clever. The evidence they planted shows great skill and knowledge of police procedure. I'm just not sure of the motive—was it to get rid of Anna or was it to steal the baby?*

*The primary suspect, in my opinion, is the baby's father, Darwin Goodman. If he wasn't instrumental in framing Thomas, he sure didn't help matters when he could have. Was he just allowing Thomas to be the convenient scapegoat, or did he plan this out?*

*Someone had to know about Anna's friendship with Thomas. And that someone had to know where the gun was located in Thomas's house. They had to lure Anna and the baby there, presuming she knew Thomas was camping. That's a question I'll have to clear with him tomorrow.*

*As soon as we get into town and let the sheriff know that Molly has escaped Thomas, we need to go to the scene of the murder. The crime lab techs have scoured the area, I'm sure, but sometimes my eyes are sharper than the humanoids'. I also have the sixth sense of the feline, which is a tremendous asset in working a case.*

*On another front, we need to stop for supplies. Thomas did the best he could with what was available, but a steady diet of corned beef will clog up my arteries and cloud my brain. I'm thinking fresh shrimp or maybe some rainbow trout. These clear mountain streams are known for the fish. I'll make sure Molly understands that fine cuisine is part of my contract. After all, I am a very discerning cat.*

*I think I'll curl up on the pillow beside Molly and take a snooze. Travel always exhausts me, and this has been one busy day. Tomorrow promises to be even busier. So, sweet dreams, my beautiful Molly. I'll wake you bright and early in the morning.*

## Chapter Five

Molly held the map Thomas had drawn for her. With the sun streaming down through the trees, the forest had changed. No longer a place of darkness and danger, it was beautiful, filled with serenity and peace.

"I'll stop here." She marked the place where Thomas had drawn a small grocery and gas station, nearly a hundred miles from the cabin. "And call the sheriff to let him know I'm okay."

"He's going to want you to come in to the sheriff's department and talk to him. It would be best if you destroyed the map," Thomas said. He stood beside her on the porch of the cabin, his hair still rumpled from sleep. He sipped a cup of black coffee and tried to look nonchalant.

She could tell he was worried—and with just cause. She held his fate in her hands. He had no transportation, little money and only enough supplies to last him for three days. "I'll be back as soon as I can." She put her hand on his arm. "Don't worry, Thomas."

"The bad thing is that worry is all I can do," he admitted. "I'm stuck here waiting while you take all the risks."

"I'll be back. If I do this, it'll increase our chances."

"I know, it's just hard to sit back and wait. Don't forget to call the office and talk to Lou Dial. He worked with Anna, too. They were friendly, and she may have made some offhand remark to him that would be a clue."

"I won't forget." Impulsively she hugged Thomas, holding him a split second longer than constituted a friendly hug. "Familiar and I will be back. I promise."

She got in the SUV, the black cat beside her, and backed away. Thomas stood on the porch, watching. He didn't wave, but his face showed his concern.

"We can't afford a mistake, Familiar," she said as she patted the map on the seat between them. "We don't have enough gas for an error."

"Meow," Familiar agreed. He put his front paws on the dash and scanned the road ahead.

With Familiar navigating, Molly felt a

whole lot better. No one would believe the feline capable of reading a map, but she no longer underestimated the black cat detective.

It was still early morning when she pulled into the gas station and filled up the vehicle. Her cell phone had no reception so she got change for the pay phone out front and dialed the sheriff.

"This is Molly Harper," she said to the clerk who answered.

"Hold for the sheriff," the young man said.

"Miss Harper," Sheriff Paul Johnson said when he came on the line. "Are you hurt? Where are you?"

"I'm headed into town," she said. "Tho— Mr. Lakeman released me and I'm perfectly fine."

There was a silence. The sheriff was not going to be as easily fooled as she'd hoped.

"Where are you?" he asked.

"Somewhere in the foothills of the mountains. I've been wandering around for most of the night, lost. But I found this little grocery and—"

"Give me the location, please."

He was irritated. She told him the name of the store and the road she was on. "How far is it to Jefferson?" she asked.

"About two hours. And you don't have a clue where you left Mr. Lakeman?"

"I'm sorry, Sheriff. I don't even know where I am. I woke up this morning in my car and he was gone. I don't know when he left or which direction he went in. I've been driving around, hoping to find some sign of civilization."

"As soon as you get into town, come by and see me."

"That's first on my list of things to do." She broke the connection before he could say anything else.

When she got back in the SUV, Familiar turned his green gaze on her.

"We're in trouble with the law, thanks to you." She reached over and patted his head. "I didn't tell you last night, but you were right about Thomas. He didn't kill Anna."

"Meow." Familiar batted the keys in the ignition.

"Okay, boy, we're headed in to beard the lions."

SHERIFF PAUL JOHNSON was a tall, lean man with a calm voice and piercing blue eyes. He sat back in his chair and eyed Molly in a way that made her skin prickle. She wasn't used to lying to authority figures—or anyone else.

"So Lakeman just got out of the car and disappeared into the wilderness somewhere."

"That's pretty much it." She felt sweat trickle down the small of her back.

"Did he have a weapon?"

Molly swallowed. "No."

"How did he convince you to leave with him?"

She thought quickly. "He came rushing out of the back of the jail and grabbed my arm. He demanded that I show him my car. When we got to the rental, he opened the door and pushed me in. I didn't really resist. I was too surprised to fight him."

"What did he say?"

She shook her head. She was walking a fine line. If she painted Thomas as some kind of dangerous abductor, things would only get worse for him. But if she acted as if she'd gone willingly, she might find herself in a cell for aiding and abetting an escape.

"He said he was innocent and that he had to prove it."

The sheriff nodded. "Everybody in jail claims to be innocent. I hope you didn't fall for that."

She shrugged. "Everything happened so fast, I didn't really think. Before I knew it, we were racing down the street with bullets flying. Once we were out of town, there wasn't a lot of conversation. He seemed intent on getting away, and I was interested only in surviving."

"You seem to have managed that." His gaze swept over her. "Not a hair out of place."

"I was lucky," she said. "Lakeman only wanted his freedom. I didn't have anything to offer."

"What about money?"

She shook her head. "I had only a hundred dollars on me, and he didn't ask for it."

"Well, we've got his accounts under surveillance and we're watching his house and friends. If he tries to get money or help, we'll nab him."

"Are you finished with me?" Molly rose.

The sheriff cast a long look at her. "For the moment. I have to say, Miss Harper, I'm not completely comfortable with the story you tell. It's beyond me why you'd assist your sister's killer in a jailbreak, but my gut instinct tells me that's exactly what happened."

"Before you make accusations, you'd better have proof." Molly forced indignation into her voice.

"Oh, proof gathering often takes time." The sheriff rose to his feet. "But time is something I have plenty of, Miss Harper. Time and tenacity. That's the backbone of good law enforcement." He nodded. "Now you have a good day."

Molly started to leave, but halfway out the door, she turned back. "I have to tell you, Sheriff, I'm not all that impressed with the efforts you've made to find my niece." She stepped closer. "My brother-in-law, a man who abused my sister, has disappeared. Do you have any leads on him?"

"Darwin Goodman isn't a suspect."

"Maybe he should be." She held her ground though her heart was pounding.

"Are you telling me how to run my investigations?" he asked.

"Do you need someone to tell you how to do it?" She was making a serious enemy. Perhaps it wasn't wise, but the sheriff had angered her. "As important as it is to find Anna's killer, it's more important to find Kate."

"There's no evidence the baby is still alive. We have our evidence and our belief is that the baby may have drowned."

If his words were meant to upset her, they

only hardened her anger. "There's no evidence she's dead." Her fingers curled around the note in her pocket. Kate was alive. She was. Molly felt it. The only thing that kept her from showing Paul Johnson the note was the implied threat that something would happen to Kate if she notified the law.

"Miss Harper, I hardly find your talents as a saleswoman enough to qualify you as a forensic expert."

The sheriff had revealed that he'd checked her background. She was, indeed, on thin ice. "My love for Anna and Kate is what qualifies me. If someone else were searching for Kate, I wouldn't have to."

"This is your first and only warning. Stay out of the way. We're going to find Lakeman and bring him in. He'll stand trial for the murder of Anna Goodman, and maybe after a few months in jail, he'll feel compelled to tell us what he did with the baby."

Molly lifted her chin to stare him down. "I'm going to find Kate. In doing so, I'll find my sister's killer. Whoever it is, they're going to be punished." She took a breath. "Whoever it is, Sheriff."

"Don't leave town, Miss Harper."

"I don't intend to leave until I have Kate

in my arms. My sister left her home to me. I'd like the key, please." But she saw from his look that Johnson had no intention of complying. She turned and left the office, her heart hammering, expecting with every step that a deputy would grab her arm and detain her. But she stepped into the February sunshine and took hurried steps toward the SUV where she could see Familiar peeking out the open window.

She got in, started the vehicle and drove away. Behind her, a patrol car pulled into the road. She was being followed, and not even with subtlety.

"I think I may have stepped in it, Familiar." She gave the cat a rundown of her conversation with the sheriff.

In fifteen minutes she found herself parked outside her sister's home. The patrol car pulled to the side of the road and parked a good distance behind her.

Molly got out, and with Familiar at her side, she walked slowly to the front door of the house that was obviously empty. Thomas had told her that Anna had left the house to her. It wasn't a crime scene and she had legal right to enter. If Anna had been planning on leaving Darwin, there might be a clue to her intended destination in the house. Such a clue might lead to Kate's whereabouts. As hard as it was going to be, she had to look.

When they were growing up, their mom had always left a spare key hidden somewhere around the back door. Molly checked around the shutters and under potted plants until she found what she sought beneath a geranium. She inserted the key in the door only to find it already unlocked. She pushed it open slowly.

THOMAS SAT AT THE TABLE and reviewed the chart he'd made. Four hours had passed since Molly had left, but it seemed like half a lifetime. The time line he was creating was an effort to account for every minute of the Friday before Anna was killed—a way of passing the time until Molly returned.

He'd worked until six o'clock Friday evening. On the drive home, he'd called a few buddies, trying to talk them into a Saturday camping trip. All had refused, saying it was too cold. But it wasn't too cold for Thomas. He loved the icy air and the winter stars over a meadow.

Had he not gone camping, could he have saved Anna?

During his stay in jail, he'd asked himself that question many times. He didn't have an answer.

He'd gotten home at six-thirty, and while he was having a drink, he'd heard a knock at the front door. Curious, he'd opened it to find a smiling Anna, baby Kate on her hip.

Surprise had been his reaction. Normally when Anna visited it was because she was scared or hurt. That night she'd had a smile that went from ear to ear.

"I'm leaving Darwin," she'd said. "Kate and I are going to build a new life. I'm going back to school."

She'd been full of plans and dreams. She'd drunk a glass of iced tea and talked, her happiness spilling over. Something had changed her, something dramatic. Thomas had asked her about it, but she'd only shaken her head and laughed. "I'm finally growing up. Molly would be proud."

She'd left, giving him a kiss on the cheek. He'd told her he would be camping but would be back Sunday evening. She'd left with a promise to see him after the weekend.

He'd closed the door, finished cooking his dinner and gone to bed early so he could rise with the sun and head for the Ozarks.

Nothing he saw or felt on Saturday morning with the weak February sun burning away the fog had prepared him for the events of that day—or what would follow. He hadn't even allowed himself time to mourn Anna's death. He'd been too busy fighting for his own freedom, trying to convince the sheriff that he was innocent.

He paced around the cabin. If Molly didn't come back, he'd head out on foot across the mountains. The sheriff had taken his cell phone. Reception was nonexistent in the mountains, anyway. Who was there to call? Not his family. His friends were certainly being watched.

He was back at the problem he'd gnawed on while in jail. The only way to prove his innocence was to find the real killer.

Darwin Goodman was the first person who popped into his head. Darwin was a hothead, a man who used his fists on a woman. He was a user and a lowlife. It was easy enough to believe he'd murdered Anna, but what Thomas couldn't figure out was what he'd done with his daughter—or why he'd taken her.

The few times Thomas had seen Darwin with the baby, it was as if the man had been charmed. He'd doted on Kate. He'd played with her and cuddled her. Could he have hidden her somewhere? Or was it possible he'd harmed—or even sold—his own child?

The answer to that was another question, How desperately did Darwin need money? That was the angle to approach it from. Did Darwin owe anybody and if so, how much?

Thomas paced the cabin, his boots striking the wooden floors. He was going crazy waiting. He went outside and found the woodpile. The ax was dull, but it would suffice to split wood and work off some of his frustrations.

THE DEPUTIES WAITED outside while Molly stepped through the unlocked door of Anna's home. Familiar went unerringly down the hall to the pale-pink room with a crib, changing table and a shelf of stuffed animals.

Molly blinked back her tears at the smell of baby lotion. It was as if Kate had been asleep in the room only moments before.

She didn't know what compelled her to search through the baby's belongings, but she did. She found several dress-up outfits, including matching shoes. But as she searched, she felt her heart lift. Nowhere in the room could she find disposable diapers or the stretch outfits so common for babies to wear. There were no baby wipes or bottles, and when she went into the kitchen, no formula in the refrigerator or the pantry.

"Familiar," she called to the cat. "Everything that Kate would need is missing. Whoever took her had the time to take all her necessities. My niece is alive, and we're going to find her."

Familiar blinked once as he nodded. He trotted out of the kitchen and into the master bedroom. Using a paw he opened the closet door to show one-half of the clothes rack empty. Only Anna's clothes remained.

Molly felt the tears well in her eyes and slip down her cheeks. She went to the clothes and touched the denim jacket that Anna had borrowed from her years before. Stitched patterns of Native American totems covered the back of the jacket, and Anna had loved it. Molly had never asked her to return it, had enjoyed the pleasure such a small thing gave her big sister.

She took the jacket from the hanger, a memento of Anna. When she looked over, Familiar was prying at the bedside table.

She went to help, but the search yielded nothing of interest. Following the cat, she moved through the house. In the den was a sideboard. It was here she found the bank statements. Technically, the papers were in her house. It was splitting hairs with the law, but she didn't have time to quibble. The papers might lead to Kate. Scooping them up, she stuffed them in her purse.

On the dining room table was a brochure for a cruise to Mexico. She took that, too. If Darwin was lurking about the Gulf of Mexico, she'd track him down and use whatever tactics necessary to find the whereabouts of Kate.

She was about to leave when Familiar snagged her pants leg and pulled her to a corner of the room.

"Good work," she said as she picked up the laptop computer. In all likelihood there wasn't anything useful on it, but if there was, she had just the man to figure out how to retrieve information. In the event Darwin might come back looking for the laptop, she left it there and made copies of every file. Those fit neatly in her large bag, too.

On the way to the back door, she stopped long enough to look up the number for another car rental agency in the phone book. Jefferson was a small town, and it would be easy enough for the sheriff to track another vehicle. But she needed only a few minutes without a tail to head back to the mountains and Thomas.

The things she'd found in the house only confirmed that Kate was alive. As long as that was true, she would endure whatever she had to, to find the baby.

And when she discovered who had taken her, that someone was going to pay dearly.

Before she left the house, she used her cell phone to call McGivens and ask for Thomas's friend, Lou. He answered on the third ring with a professional greeting.

"I'm a friend of Thomas Lakeman," she said, not even bothering to identify herself. "He needs your help."

"What can I do?"

Lou didn't beat around the bush, and she liked that. "Did Anna mention anyone to you? Any new friends? Any plans? Anything that might help Thomas find the real killer?"

"Who are you?" Lou asked. Suspicion had crept into his voice.

"I'm Anna's sister. Molly Harper."

"You're the woman Thomas abducted from the jail yesterday? You're trying to help him?"

Molly wanted to beat the telephone against

the wall. She didn't have time to persuade and convince people. She needed answers. "Thomas is innocent. I'm trying to help him. Can you help me to do that?"

"We all know Thomas wouldn't hurt Anna, but she didn't say anything to me. I wish I could be more helpful, but I don't know anything."

Molly felt defeated. "Try to think. I'll call you back later."

"Where are you? Where's Thomas?"

"It's best for you not to know anything." She hung up. In this situation, for Lou ignorance was bliss.

Next she called the rental agency, requesting the delivery of a car at a service station she'd passed three blocks from Anna's house. She checked the front window and saw the patrol car down the block. As long as her car was in the driveway, they wouldn't suspect she was gone until it was too late.

"Come on, Familiar," she said as she slipped out the back door and ran toward the fence she'd have to scale.

THOMAS DIDN'T RECOGNIZE the headlights of the vehicle that pulled into the drive of the cabin. His first impulse was to take to the woods, but he held his ground. There was a chance he could bluff his way through. He knew the owner of the cabin, and if this was a friend come to check on the place, he could win them over.

The woman who got out of the pickup was slender, her hair tumbled about her shoulders. It wasn't until he saw the silhouette of the cat as he darted through the lamplight to the door that Thomas really believed it was Molly and Familiar.

"How did you get back so quickly?" He was delighted and didn't try to hide it. "I've been going stir-crazy. Did you find anything? What happened? Was the sheriff suspicious?" He had a million questions, but mostly he wanted to look at Molly. There was something different about her. Along with the sadness, there was a new light in her eyes.

"I ditched the deputy who was following me." Molly's eyes almost danced. "Kate is alive. I know it for sure." She told him what she'd found at the house.

"I think you're right," he said. He grasped her arms and hugged her to him. She was so slender, so delicate, but her heartbeat was strong and vital. He could feel it against his chest, and it was one of the most remarkable things he'd ever felt.

"I've been worried sick about Kate," Molly said, her arms wrapped around him. "But she's okay. We're going to find her."

He was relieved. Concerns about the baby had tormented him all day. Molly's revelations, though, made him feel for certain that Kate was alive. Somewhere. "We'll find her, and we'll find Anna's killer. That's a promise. I'll go over those financial records and we need to find a computer to look at those files you copied."

# Chapter Six

*Grilled rainbow trout is about the best a cat can expect—especially when it's just pulled from a clear mountain stream. I have to give Thomas credit for his culinary abilities. He caught the trout earlier today just for me. He said he had to have something to do to pass the time. I'll give him a little sandpaper tongue for his efforts. Hmm, he's not certain how to take a kitty kiss.*

*The bipeds have cleaned up the dishes and started working on the financial statements. The computer files will have to wait until Molly can secure a laptop. I think I'll take a tiny little nap. It's been a tough two days for a feline detective. Hurtled through the air in a plane, half-starved on canned corned beef, exhausted from planning and executing prison breaks. I feel the need for a nap.*

*I'll curl up right here on the sofa and keep*

*an eye on the humanoids. There are definite sparks between them, though neither of them wants to admit it. From my vantage point, I can see they're perfect for each other, but it always takes the bipeds a bit longer to suss out the truth about love. It's amazing how the species has taken over the planet with all of the difficulty they have finding romance.*

*But that's a problem for another day. I'll just snuggle down into this comforter and sleep. Ah, the rewards of a clear conscience.*

"HERE'S SOMETHING." Molly held up the January bank statement that showed a ten-thousand-dollar deposit. "Where would Darwin and Anna get that kind of money?"

She could see by the expression in Thomas's eyes that he thought the worst, as she did. When he didn't say anything, she asked the question she could no longer avoid. "Do you really believe Darwin killed Anna so he could sell his own child?"

Thomas took a long breath. "I don't know. If you'd asked me that a week ago, I would've said no. I would've told you that Darwin is a coward and a bully, but that he cares for Kate. Still, she's missing, and there's money in his account and no one is showing much of an interest in finding Kate or real evidence that she met foul play."

"Why hasn't the sheriff checked into this?" Molly slapped the table. "What's wrong with everyone?"

Thomas rose from the computer and walked over to her. He sat down beside her, his hand closing lightly over her fingers. "Either Sheriff Johnson truly believes I'm guilty, or he's incompetent, or he's involved. Of those three options, I hope it's number two."

"If he's in this—"

"It's going to complicate everything a lot." Thomas rubbed his face where a two-day growth of beard had given him the rugged look of a range hand. "That was quick thinking on your part to change rental cars. I'll bet those deputies are still sitting outside, wondering what you're doing."

"You can be sure Sheriff Johnson has checked my legal right to be in the house."

"You bought us a little time, but we need to move fast if we're going to investigate."

"Why don't we do the thing they would least expect?" Molly said. "Why don't we move into Darwin and Anna's house? If it was the place she was killed, I couldn't do it, but Anna's house must have held many pleasant memories of Kate." She could see he was impressed with her suggestion.

"It's probably the one place they wouldn't look for us, and the computer is there," he conceded.

"Anna had to have left something behind for us to find, some indication of her plans. When we were kids, we'd pretend that we were twins and that we knew each other's thoughts. We'd hide things in secret places for each other."

"Anna was always secretive, but don't get your hopes up." He squeezed her arm. "I'll help you search the house again, but you know the police must have conducted a thorough search."

"Sometimes you have to trust your heart, not your eyes." She was determined. "Up here we're isolated, which also means we can't really investigate. We need to be close to town."

Thomas nodded. "You're right."

"It's more dangerous for you, but—"

"The advantages outweigh the danger. We'll head there tonight."

"Anna told me I was always welcome." Molly felt the sadness touch her. "I had no idea she'd leave her house to me. I'll probably have to sell it, but I can guarantee the proceeds will go toward Kate's education."

"Anna knew you'd do the right thing, and she couldn't trust Darwin to." He picked up the few belongings they'd brought into the cabin. "Let's hit it. Tomorrow we can try to trace that bank deposit. I need an Internet hookup to do it."

"Good thinking."

"If someone wiped the hard drive, there are things I can do to reconstruct it, but I need to be able to tap into my office to download some software."

She felt exhaustion hit her like a wall, and sank onto the sofa. Beside her, Familiar was curled in a kitty comma, the tip of his tail barely flicking in a dream. "I feel like I've stepped into a nightmare and can't wake up."

"Talk about something pleasant. Tell me how you ended up living on an Indian reservation." Thomas eased onto the sofa near her.

Molly had long ago realized there wasn't a simple answer to that question. The first part of the story was easy, and she told it as she stared into the fire.

She'd first moved to Santa Fe to work and live in a community of artists. One day she'd gotten lost while looking for an herb shop.

Instead, she'd found an elderly woman selling the most exquisite jewelry she'd ever seen.

"I knew instantly that if this jewelry were marketed properly, it would become the 'must have' accessory for the fashionable. In that moment my entire life changed. I no longer saw myself as an artist, but rather as a person who had been sent to help expose the art of this woman to the world. I packed up and moved to Arizona to live on the reservation."

"Did you have marketing skills?"

"From long ago, when I worked for an advertising agency. I never imagined I'd actually enjoy doing marketing and public relations, but I've been consumed by it. I owe my new life to the artist Martha Whitedove." She could see that Thomas knew the name.

"Every woman I work with has talked about her jewelry," he said. "I wouldn't exactly say that I'm in touch with the fashion world, but I know of her work. It's been featured in several area magazines. Anna turned several of my co-workers on to her jewelry and they talked about it all the time." Thomas got up and poured them each a cup of coffee.

"Martha's incredible. And she's not the only one. There are weavers and dye makers.

The reservation has so much talent, and the people are so poor. I want to make a difference. I'm going to make a difference."

Instead of laughing at her, Thomas lifted his cup in a toast. "I have no doubt you will, Molly. You already have."

"For the past few years, I was so consumed by my work at the reservation that I neglected Anna." Here was the downside of her work.

"Anna didn't feel neglected. Obviously you e-mailed each other. Whenever I talked with her, she had news about what you were doing. She told me a few weeks ago that you'd sent her something new for Katie's crib."

Molly frowned. "But I didn't. I sent her a dream catcher."

Thomas waved his hand. "I must have confused something she said. Go on, please. Tell me about being Anna's sister."

Molly sighed, feeling the weight of regret. "We stayed in touch, but I didn't visit often. I came when Kate was born, but I never liked Darwin. He made me uncomfortable, and Anna was ill at ease whenever I was there. I see now Darwin made it a point to make me feel unwelcome." She felt the bitterness rise up. "It's hard to bully your wife in front of company."

"How are you handling your job?"

"I just finished the spring catalog, so I have a few weeks off. I'd planned on coming here to Jefferson to visit Anna and Kate, but Anna was murdered before I could finalize my plans." She shook her head. "I'd hoped to convince my sister to bring the baby back home with me for a visit. There's an artist on the reservation. I wanted him to do a portrait of them."

So many plans would never bear fruit now. Molly knew she would feel the loss of her sister for the rest of her life. Kate's disappearance was like a hole in her future.

"You can't give up on the baby," Thomas urged her.

She shook her head. "Not a chance." She pulled the note from her pocket and read it again. "I know Kate is alive. Someone is trying to guide me to her, but I feel I'm not following the clues very well. I just have to keep trying, though."

"We'll keep trying together," Thomas said, touching her hand.

THE FIRE WAS DYING and Thomas burrowed deeper beneath the quilts on the sofa. Familiar had opted to sleep with him, and he was glad of it. The cat was a small furnace, tucked at his chin. He'd been around plenty of dogs but never cats. And certainly never a cat like Familiar.

How was it that such a remarkable cat and woman had entered his life on the same day?

As much as he enjoyed thinking about Molly, he forced his thoughts to what he'd discovered in the bank statements. He hadn't told Molly, and that scalded him. He'd kept his silence for several reasons, the most important being an effort to protect Molly. He didn't want to raise her hopes of finding Kate. For the four months prior to Anna's murder, an electronic transfer of funds to the tune of thirty thousand dollars from a Cayman Island bank had been paid to the Goodmans' joint account.

In mid-January, a draft on the account had been drawn and paid to Paradise Real Estate in Brownsville, Texas. Thomas wanted to make the call before he told Molly and got her hopes up.

The cat stirred and gazed at him.

It was almost as if Familiar were warning him not to get too worked up. Thomas forced his body to relax. There wasn't anything he could do until they got to town where he'd have the Internet and the resources of his job.

THOMAS WAS ON THE FLOORBOARD of the car when Molly pulled up the driveway to Anna's home and parked behind the house. It was 4:00 a.m., and the sheriff's car that had been parked outside when she left was gone. By now the sheriff would have figured out that she'd given his men the slip. She didn't relish the thought of her next meeting with Johnson. She wasn't a suspect exactly, but the sheriff wouldn't be happy with her conduct.

She got her purse from the back of the car and called Familiar to follow as she walked to the front door. As she pushed the door open, she saw a patrol car pull up at the curb. She entered the house, flipping on the lights, ignoring the deputies outside. She anticipated a knock, but when none came, she had to force her shoulders to relax.

She was nervous about Thomas. If the deputies thoroughly searched the car, they'd find him, even though he was hidden under her bags. There was nothing she could do, except act as normal as possible. She unlocked the back door and cracked it open, part of the plan she'd concocted with Thomas.

In the guest bathroom she ran a hot tub. Even anxious and worried, she smiled at the prospect of a bath. She felt as if it had been a year since she'd had the convenience of indoor plumbing. It was truly one of the marks of a civilized society.

She took her bath, dressed in clean clothes, wrapped a towel around her wet hair and prepared two cups of hot chocolate for the deputies. She took them out to the car, chatting for a moment, thanking them for watching out for her, giving Thomas time to slip from the car, through the backyard and into the house.

When she returned to the house, he was in the guest bathroom, the shower running. She wasn't the only one who admired indoor plumbing.

When he came out, they sat at the kitchen table, the gray light of dawn showing through the drawn shades. "I'm as much a prisoner here as at the jail," he said.

"Not quite."

"We have to shake that tail."

"If I leave, they'll follow me." Molly had given it some thought. "I'll call the rental company and use my business account. They'll deliver a car wherever you say."

His smile was wry. "You're a better criminal than I am, Molly."

"I have many talents," she said.

The shrill ring of the house telephone made both of them freeze. Molly walked to the counter and picked up the phone. Her gaze holding onto Thomas's, she said hello.

"Stop meddling or you'll pay the price." The voice was mechanical, as if it came through a synthesizer, which only made it more terrifying.

Thomas was at her side in an instant. "Who's on the phone?" he mouthed.

The line went dead.

Molly felt as if a freezing wind had chilled her to the bone. When Thomas put his arms around her, she clung to the warmth of his chest.

"What did they say?" he asked.

"The person threatened me. It was one of those mechanical voices, and I couldn't tell if it was male or female, but it said that if I didn't stop meddling I'd pay the price."

Thomas's hands moved up and down her arms and back bringing warmth back to her. He hugged her tight against him.

"Listen to me, Molly, this is good news. They wouldn't threaten you if you weren't bothering them. We haven't even begun to search, but they're aware we're on their trail.

We have them on the offensive, and that's where we're going to keep them."

"How?"

"They're watching you. They knew you were here. That's given them something to chew on." His voice took on an edge. "You get the threatening phone call when you're here, at Anna's. Maybe there is something here they're afraid we'll find. Maybe the caller was Darwin."

"It could have been. We don't know where he is." She was suddenly tired and afraid.

"I think I can find him."

Molly eased back so she could look into Thomas's eyes. For the briefest second she glimpsed his anger and his pain. The one thing she had to keep in mind was that Thomas Lakeman was a master of self-control.

"I'm so sorry for all you've been through," she said. "I've lost my sister and niece, but you've lost plenty, too."

"You have my word that I won't stop until we find out what happened to Kate," he said.

She had no reason to doubt he meant it. "We'll find my niece *and* prove your innocence."

"After seeing that note and finding the financial documents here in this house, I believe Kate is alive. It's more important to find her than it is to worry about my legal problems."

Molly touched his cheek. "I don't know if I could do this alone."

"You don't have to. Whatever happens to me, I'll do my best to find Kate."

THOMAS STOOD BESIDE the sofa and watched the rise and fall of Molly's chest as if he'd never seen another person breathe. She was amazing. She came across as so cool and collected, so sophisticated. Exhaustion had finally claimed her and she'd fallen asleep curled on the sofa with Familiar beside her.

Certainly, he'd fantasized about Molly. She was a beautiful woman who could inspire any man to such thoughts, but now wasn't the time for romance. In the soft morning light, he looked at her. She was extraordinary, and for the first time since he'd met her, she looked peaceful.

He slipped into the small office where the Goodmans' computer was set up. While she slept, he wanted to do an intensive search of the files. If he could find some clue that could prove his suspicions, his best bet might be to go to the sheriff—even though he didn't trust the man. Surely with rock-solid evidence, Johnson would be forced to drop the charges against Thomas. He wanted to be free of the false charge so he could focus totally on finding Kate. This was something he wanted to do for Molly and for Anna. Something no one else could do as well as he could. And he didn't want to be hamstrung by a bunch of deputies on his tail.

He opened the computer on the table and plugged it into the phone jack. Using the skills he'd learned at work, he began the tedious task of reconstructing files.

Darwin's e-mail account had been wiped, but Thomas was able to pull up old messages. Darwin had been corresponding with someone, talking about "the package," a payment and a delivery date—the very day Anna was killed and Kate disappeared. The e-mails weren't solid proof, but the anger in Thomas's gut told him Darwin was somehow involved. His fists clenched, and he had the almost intolerable desire to punch Darwin as many times as it took to beat the truth out of him.

The sound of a door creaking open caught his attention but not fast enough. Something stiff and black was pulled over his head.

Thomas struggled, lashing out and striking the solid chest of his adversary. He tried to call out to Molly, to warn her that an intruder was in the house. But before he could cry out, something struck him.

He went down to his knees. The noise he heard next was like nothing he'd ever imagined. It was a shriek of fury. He had no idea where it came from.

"Damn," his assailant cried before he let go of his hold on Thomas.

Thomas dragged off the cloth sack that had been pulled over his head and saw the broad back of a man running out the back door. Familiar was right on his heels, his fur fluffed out and a roar of anger coming from his throat.

Before the man could clear the door, Familiar was on him, leaping high on his back and digging his claws into his neck.

"Get off!" The man spun in a circle and tried to slam the cat into the door frame, but Familiar was too quick. He leaped to safety and the man ran out the door.

Thomas staggered to his feet, grasping the table for support. The blow had almost knocked him unconscious.

Molly, holding a butcher knife, ran into the room. "What happened?"

"Someone attacked us," Thomas said.

"With two deputies sitting out front?" Molly went to the front window and looked out. "They're still there. We should report this."

Thomas eased into a chair. His head was throbbing and he could taste iron in the back of his mouth where he'd bitten his tongue. "No. I'm getting a real bad feeling about law enforcement in Jefferson County."

Molly let the drapery fall back into place. "That would explain why Sheriff Johnson didn't investigate Kate's disappearance." Excitement was in her voice.

"It would explain a lot. Molly, there's something else going on here beyond a domestic argument that turned violent."

"What do you think it is?"

"I honestly don't know yet. But we'll find out. The good news is there must be something in this house worth them taking a big risk. Now we're going to find it."

## *Chapter Seven*

Molly was amazed that something as hard as Thomas's head could bleed so much. She applied the bandage she'd found in the bathroom medicine cabinet without comment. He needed stitches, but nothing she said could convince him to seek medical care. He was determined not to go to the hospital.

When she stepped back from cleaning the wound to his head, she realized he was staring at her. For a second neither spoke, both too aware of the rush of emotion that connected them almost like an electrical arc. She wanted to look away but couldn't.

She broke the moment. "Thomas, you need to get medical care. I've done the best I can, but I have no way to tell if there was serious damage."

"I'm not that stubborn, Molly. But if I go to the hospital emergency room, it's likely the nursing staff will call the sheriff's department." He looked at his hands as he spoke.

"It's a head wound, not a gunshot. Why would they report it?" She took a breath, glad that Thomas was ignoring the moment that had just passed between them.

He shook his head gently. "I can't risk it."

She sat on the arm of the sofa. Thomas was right. Now that the bleeding had stopped, the wound wasn't as bad as she first thought. "Okay, but you need some antibiotic salve."

"That's a reasonable compromise," he said. "Before we do anything, we need to find what the guy was looking for." The black cat rubbed against his shins, and Thomas bent down to pick him up.

Familiar held up a paw and Molly saw that something was hung there. Leaning forward, she pulled the tuft of green fleece out of his claws. "Look at this. Familiar has evidence from our assailant."

She held the tuft of material out so Thomas could examine it.

"Hunter-green polar fleece." Thomas touched it. "Feels like it came from an expensive jacket."

"Did you get a look at the attacker?"

"No. The man was on me before I even knew what was happening. He slugged me from behind, and the only thing I saw after that was the floor rising up to meet me."

"What I don't understand is why he would come in here *knowing* someone was here. The car is parked in the driveway, but he came right in anyway." Molly stood up and began to pace. "Like he didn't care that someone was here."

"He knew *you* were here," Thomas pointed out. "He didn't expect me, and I certainly don't think he anticipated Familiar. He gave the guy some serious wounds."

"Good. He got what he deserved." Molly had never thought she was the kind of woman who would enjoy revenge, but she was learning new things about herself. "The intruder thought I was here alone, so he didn't hesitate to break in." Even saying the words aloud made her stomach knot. This person had killed her sister and likely had Kate. He wouldn't hesitate to hurt her.

"That's how I read it."

"What could he have wanted?"

"That's what we have to find out, and quickly. Do you have any idea?" he asked.

Molly shook her head. "There has to be something here."

Thomas rose slowly to his feet, weaving slightly. He gained his balance and gave her a determined look. "The man was bold, the way he came in. As if he didn't fear the consequences of what he was about to do, which makes me wonder again with two deputies outside. Let's see what's in this house that he wanted."

Molly took his hand. "Take it easy, Thomas. I'm not sure you need to be searching for anything. How about you take a seat and I'll hunt—with Familiar's help, of course."

She saw how much it cost him to relax, but Thomas eased back down on the sofa. His face was pale, his forehead beaded with sweat. He'd been hit a lot harder than he wanted to admit.

He swallowed and rubbed his forehead. "Maybe you're right. That guy really clobbered me."

"You can direct the search from the sofa. I'm going to start in the bathroom," she said. "While I'm at it, I'll bring you some aspirin. It might help that headache."

His smile moved slowly across his face. "You're too smart for your own good."

"It doesn't take a genius to see the goose egg on your head and then figure you've got a headache. I'll be back. Come on, Familiar." She moved down the hall with the cat at her side. She paused to look at a painting hanging on the wall. The trial of Geronimo. She'd painted it for Anna when she was in college, when Molly thought her path in life was to be a painter. Anna had loved it, even though Molly could clearly see how amateurish her work had been.

She sighed and followed the cat down the hall. In the bathroom, Familiar pawed open the cabinet doors and began his investigation while she removed the towels and washcloths from the top cabinet. In five minutes they knew the bathroom contained nothing that would help them—except the aspirin for Thomas. Molly took them to him with a glass of water.

"Maybe the guest room," he suggested.

"It would help if I had some clue as to what I'm looking for."

He considered. "The police have looked through the house, so it has to be something they missed."

"Smaller than a breadbox…" She rolled her eyes.

"Molly, there's something you should think about. If I weren't here with you, you could report this break-in to the sheriff. We don't have any clear evidence that connects Johnson with anything illegal going on."

"To be honest, I get a bad feeling when I talk to the sheriff." She bit her bottom lip. "I had a feeling that Anna was in trouble, and I didn't act on it soon enough. If I'd visited two weeks before, maybe none of this would have happened."

"I disagree about changing the course of events. As much as I want to believe Darwin is behind this, I can't make the pieces fit together. There's something else going on, and I don't think your presence here would have been a factor."

Molly turned away to shield her emotions. "Why isn't the sheriff hunting for Kate? Why didn't he call in the FBI? What's going on here?"

"The one thing I know about Johnson is that he was mighty quick to pin the murder on me."

"Meow!" Familiar stood in the hallway, pacing in a circle.

Thomas nodded at the cat. "We have something better than a secret weapon. We have Familiar."

Molly squared her shoulders. "Right, and he's ready to reexamine the rest of the house."

Familiar led the way into the guest bedroom and began a methodical search while she helped the cat and considered what Sheriff Paul Johnson's role might be in everything that had happened to her family.

The chest of drawers and closet were as empty as the answers she came up with regarding the sheriff of Jefferson County. The bottom line was that she couldn't trust Johnson or his men. She and Thomas and Familiar were on their own.

"Finding anything?" Thomas called.

"This room looks like no one ever used it. The sheets are still brand-new."

Familiar walked into the hallway and looked back at her. "Meow." It was an order.

"I'm coming." She followed the cat down the hallway and into the baby's room. Molly stopped in the doorway, caught by a sudden rush of emotion. Kate should be in her bed, snoozing. By all rights Anna should be standing beside the crib.

"Meow!" Familiar moved to the crib. He stretched his front paws up and began to claw at the wood.

Molly's first thought was to stop him, but she realized Familiar never acted without reason. Something about the crib wasn't right. She remembered what Thomas had said—Anna told him she'd sent something for the baby's bed. But she hadn't. Anna had e-mailed her about a new type of mattress that was safer, but Molly hadn't been involved in purchasing it. Thinking back over the e-mails, Molly realized how strange they were in tone. Almost as if Anna were sending one of the secret clues they'd left each other as children.

She stepped to the crib and looked it over. A pink-and-yellow coverlet with cartoon characters covered the pale-yellow flannel sheets. A stuffed giraffe and panda were at the foot of the bed. It all looked so sweet and innocent that she blinked back tears.

Familiar hopped into the crib, walking back and forth as if he were testing the mattress. In the center of the crib he stopped and turned to her.

"Meow." He kneaded the mattress with his claws.

Molly pulled back the sheets. The mattress looked brand-new. "What?" she asked the cat.

He dug his claws into the mattress. "Meow!" His tone was insistent. He went to the edge of the mattress and began to pull at a corner as if he meant to remove the mattress.

Molly grasped the mattress and tugged. If Familiar wanted to dismantle the bed, she'd help him. As she removed the mattress, Familiar jumped to the floor.

Putting her arms around the mattress to put it back, she felt something hard. She turned the small mattress on its side, examining the seams. As she worked her way around it, she came to a place where the stitching was different. Using a pair of baby nail scissors from the bedside table, she cut the mattress open.

Reaching her hand inside, she felt a small leather-bound notebook. "What is this?" she asked as she maneuvered it through the hole she'd made. Familiar sat beside her, tail twitching, as she pulled the notebook free of the mattress. *Kate's Book* was written on the front of it.

Molly sank to the floor and opened the notebook. She recognized her sister's handwriting instantly. As she flipped the pages, she realized it was a journal of Anna's pregnancy, the most intimate of moments that a mother could write to her child. But why had she hidden it in a mattress, risking that it might not be found?

The last entry stopped Molly cold. It was

dated just a few days after Anna's birth. The flowing script of her sister's hand said, "I'm telling you this now, Katie, even though you won't understand it. I don't ever want there to be secrets between us, and this is important for you to know if anything should happen to me. Darwin isn't your father. Your dad is a good man, a loving man who would claim you if he could. One day, when you're older and he's not afraid for our safety, we'll be with him. One day we'll change our lives—that's the promise I make to you now, when you've just entered the world. I'm trusting that your aunt Molly will find this and tell you when the time is right."

Molly closed the notebook. Of all the things she'd expected, it wasn't to discover that her sister had had an affair. She thought of Thomas, his closeness with Anna. His desire to protect her. Was it something more than friendship? It was a question she had to ask. Her feelings for Thomas were changing. If he'd been involved with Anna, she needed to know.

"Molly, did you find something?"

Thomas's voice came from the living room. She rose, notebook in hand. "Yes," she said. "Familiar found it. You're not going to believe it, though." She walked to the living room and handed him the journal. "Read the last entry."

She watched his face until he finished and looked up at her, amazed. "I had no idea."

"Then you aren't Kate's father?"

"No," Thomas said, unoffended by the question. "She's a wonderful baby, but she isn't mine. Anna and I didn't have that type of feeling for each other."

Molly felt a weight lift from her heart. She believed Thomas. Maybe she was a fool, but she did believe him. "Any idea who Kate's father might be?"

Thomas tapped his hand on the sofa. "None. Anna never mentioned another man. Not one single time." He stood slowly, the notebook in his hand. "This is another kettle of fish. I mean this could be motive for Darwin to…" He didn't finish.

"Do you think Darwin found this out, killed Anna in a fit of jealous anger, and then gave Kate away because she wasn't his baby?"

Thomas walked to the windows and looked out. "I suppose that's possible, but it just doesn't seem right. Why didn't she simply leave Darwin if she loved someone else? Darwin had gone through all of her money. She and the baby were obligations for him to take care of. He might have let her go without a fight. He didn't strike me as the kind of man who liked being encumbered by a wife and kid." He looked at her. "I honestly thought Anna loved Darwin. This is hard for me to accept."

Molly pinched the bridge of her nose with her fingers. "It would seem that neither of us knew my sister. Really knew her. That's going to make it doubly hard to find Kate and prove your innocence."

THOMAS WATCHED as Molly drove away, headed to the sheriff's office and to run some errands—essentially to make herself visible. They'd decided to wait until dark to try to get into Thomas's house.

Familiar had gone with Molly—and Thomas was amused that he felt the cat could protect her. In just a couple of days he'd become a convert to the Familiar fan club. The cat was a dynamo, no doubt about it.

He sat down at the computer and went back to work, pulling up records that Darwin Goodman had thought were permanently erased. He came upon another e-mail that intrigued him. "The cash is in your account. Now deliver the package."

When Thomas tried to trace the e-mail address, he found the account was closed. To pursue it further might raise suspicions, and Thomas didn't know if the law was onto this lead. He doubted it, but he decided to back off. Of more importance was what was happening in Darwin's bank account right now.

With the software he'd downloaded he was able to break into Darwin's online banking records at Jefferson National Bank. There was no additional information on the thirty thousand dollars that had been paid into the account. No matter how he tried to trace the funds, he ended up at a roadblock. The accounts were untraceable with the equipment he had.

He moved on to Darwin's spending habits. "Bingo," he said to himself as he found a pen and jotted down the fact that Darwin had drafted a check to the Tumbleweed Inn in Brownsville, Texas, the week before. That, plus the check that Darwin had written to Paradise Real Estate in Brownsville told Thomas that Brownsville was the next destination for Molly and him. There was a chance that Darwin had started a new life there, a life with Kate. Or more likely, with the amount of money Darwin had put into the account, that he'd done something with the baby girl once he'd learned she wasn't his own.

A movement outside the house made him get up and go to the window. Easing the curtain back just an inch he looked out. Molly was back. He was completely unprepared for the desire that swept over him as he watched her get out of the car and walk toward the house. She was beautiful, the type of woman he'd never have met in either his career as a cowboy or computer programmer. She had class and style and heart. And he had nothing to offer her, not even dinner at a nice restaurant. He was a fugitive. A man wanted for murder.

But once the baby was safe and his name was cleared, he intended to pay court to Molly Harper.

MOLLY WATCHED the play of emotions in Thomas's face as he spoke. He'd discovered something while she was gone, and it was going to be upsetting.

"I found out where Darwin is. Brownsville. I think we should go there. I think he's creating a new life for himself, a new identity."

"With Kate?" She was ready to fly out the door.

Thomas hesitated. "In going over his financial records, I found several large payments of untraceable cash in his checking account for a total of nearly thirty thousand dollars. I can't figure where he got that kind of money."

"Unless he sold Kate because she wasn't his." Molly felt her stomach knot. A cash deal for a baby would be hard to track down if Darwin wouldn't talk. They had to find him and force him to tell what he knew.

"Let's find him and confront him." Molly felt eagerness and dread.

"I suggest a more patient approach. We need to watch him. He's our only link to Kate's possible whereabouts."

"If he realizes Kate isn't his daughter, we might not have time." If Kate was no blood kin to Darwin, would he feel anything for the baby? If he didn't feel he had a personal interest in Kate, he was capable of anything.

"Let's get on the road and see what we can find out about Darwin and his activities." Thomas put his hand on her arm.

It was a gesture of comfort and support. Molly knew that but his touch warmed her heart. "Thomas, we can't let him harm Kate."

"Kate is alive," he assured her. His hand moved up to rub the taut muscles of her neck. "She's alive and we're going to find her. With Familiar and me on your team, you can't fail, Molly."

Thomas's support was so generously given, and so sincere. Molly found she couldn't speak. The lump in her throat was too large. She turned to face him and saw that he understood.

"Darwin might be a creep and a wife abuser, but we have no evidence that he would harm a child. Keep that in mind."

Molly finally managed to gain control of her voice. "That's right. We'll find her."

"We'll go to Brownsville as soon as we check out my place." Thomas's gaze searched her face.

She nodded, looking away. She wasn't used to a man who so openly showed his concern for her. "As soon as it's dark, we'll head to your home." She took a deep breath. "By the way, when I stopped by the courthouse, Sheriff Johnson said he pulled the deputies off surveillance. I'm no longer suspected of being an accomplice in your jailbreak."

"When pigs fly," Thomas said.

She smiled. "Indeed. When pigs fly."

## *Chapter Eight*

Molly and Familiar got out of the rental car two blocks from Thomas's house. They'd let him out on the block behind his home. His intention was to cut through several back-yards and approach his residence in a quiet, older part of town by scaling the back fence.

As she drove toward the cottage-style house with a wraparound porch, Molly's dread tripled. This was going to be the hardest part of all. The prospect of seeing the place where her sister had died was almost more than she could bear. But if the police had overlooked the diary hidden in Kate's crib, what might they have failed to see at the murder scene? Familiar needed to examine the scene, and Molly intended to be there with him. The sheriff's forensic team had acquired as much evidence as they needed to pin the murder on Thomas, so the house was no longer part of an active crime scene.

She'd been careful, watching for a tail, but as far as she could see there wasn't one. Sheriff Johnson had lost interest in her, or so it would seem. She didn't trust the lawman, though, and she didn't want to lead the police to Thomas. To that end, she parked a block away and moved swiftly through the shadows toward her destination.

As she eased down the sidewalk, Familiar at her side, Molly took note of her surroundings. She was in an old residential neighborhood with a scattering of two-story homes, bungalows and ranch-style brick. Tree roots disrupted a sidewalk that was meant for children or bicycles and skates. So different from Anna's street, which was a cul-de-sac with new brick homes on either side, the lawns so perfect they seemed fake. This was a real neighborhood, not some developer's idea of compatible theme housing.

At the walkway lined with boxwoods that led to Thomas's gracious porch and front door, she paused. She felt Familiar at her ankles as he pressed against her and purred, lending the support that she needed so much. She took a deep breath and followed the cat up the walk and to the door. She twisted the knob and felt it give. The door opened on the whisper of a touch.

She knew instantly that Thomas was in the room. She felt his presence before she made out his silhouette in the glow of a streetlight coming through an unshaded window.

"We shouldn't turn on any lights," he said.

"I know." She pulled a high-intensity flashlight from her pocket. "I bought a couple of these today. I thought they might come in handy."

"You would've made one heckuva Girl Scout." He took the light. "Are you sure you want to do this?"

She looked around for the cat, and when she didn't see him, she knew Familiar was already examining the scene where Anna had been killed.

"I don't want to, but I have to. If there's any evidence that might lead us to Kate, I have to see it. I have to—" Despite her best efforts, her voice broke.

Thomas moved silently across the dark room. His arms went around her and he held her, and for the first time since she'd learned of her sister's death, she felt safe enough to relax.

"I wish I could change this for you." His voice was whisper-soft, but there was strength in his words.

For one brief moment she yielded to her grief. His arms tightened around her, holding her, as her sobs shook her. She felt the softness of his cotton shirt against her cheek. She could hear his heart thump and knew that he would hold her for as long as it took.

The storm of grief passed quickly. There wasn't time to indulge her heartache. She sighed and pulled herself together, and his hold loosened.

"I'm sorry," she said. "I haven't grieved Anna's death properly. I've been so focused on finding Kate."

"And helping me clear my name. I can see how difficult it is for you to show your grief to another person. I'm glad it's me." He stepped back. "Before you go into the bedroom, let me look first."

She didn't resist his effort to protect her. This was one time if Thomas wanted to take the brunt of horror, she would let him. Although she listened for his progress through the house, she didn't hear anything. Even in the dark, he maneuvered soundlessly through his own home. She waited in the living room, looking out the window on a street that looked like a scene from an old black-and-white movie when the world was safe.

"Molly, are you sure about this?" Thomas called to her.

Once she was away from the window, she clicked on her flashlight. She moved down a hallway until she came to an open door and saw the glow of Thomas's light. At the doorway she steeled herself for whatever lay in front of her.

Her light swept the room, the beam touching a bed neatly made, solid oak furniture, pale walls and a beige carpet. The room was neat. The bedside tables were not cluttered as her sister's had been. Mollie's flashlight beam swung down and she found the chalk outline of her sister's body, the blood that had soaked the carpet. She looked at the blood for a long time, then her light moved up to Thomas's face.

He stood by the bed, his gaze on hers, his expression worried. "Are you sure you're okay?"

"Yes." The beam swung down and found Familiar as he paced from the doorway to the body's outline. He repeated his actions, looking up at her and meowing as he did so.

The cat always had a reason for his actions, even if she didn't understand. "Thomas, do you know what he's trying to tell us?"

"That Anna was *in* the bedroom when she was shot. Whoever shot her was in the *hallway*."

Molly thought about the implications of that. "What does that tell you?"

"I think Anna came here because she was scared. She came to the safest place she could think of—my room. Maybe she was hiding in the closet." Thomas went to the closet and opened the door. His light traced the small room, showing where shirts and pants had been pushed aside. "Someone was here. Whether it was Anna or the police, I can't say."

"If she was hiding, where was Kate?"

"I can't answer that."

Molly felt her heart leap. "Anna would never leave Kate. She wouldn't leave her baby. If she was here, Kate was, too. If the killer had murdered her, Johnson would have found her body."

"I want to agree with you, Molly, but we both realize we didn't truly know Anna. Maybe she took Kate somewhere safe. Then she came here to hide and waited for me to come home. Maybe she thought I could help her." He made a noise of frustration. "Damn it. Suppositions are worse than nothing. We can develop a thousand scenarios of what Anna was doing and why, and none of them will help us until we find some evidence."

Molly clicked off her flashlight. "Grab the things you think you'll need and let's get out of here."

"I couldn't agree more." Thomas pulled a suitcase from the closet and hastily began to throw clean clothes in it. "I want to get some equipment from my office, then I'll be ready." He handed her the suitcase. "I'll meet you at the car. Let's head to Brownsville and see if we can get some answers out of Darwin."

ONCE THEY CLEARED Dallas, Molly slept. Thomas, with Familiar riding shotgun, drove through the dark morning hours and into the dawn.

In the soft light, Molly looked younger. Her face was relaxed, innocent, he thought as he glanced at her. She was such a strange combination of vulnerability and strength. The memory of her in his arms came unbidden. He felt a rush of emotion and desire as he remembered his hands moving over her strong, lean back, pressing her tight against him. It was impossible to keep such thoughts at bay all the time, but he realized that Molly needed a friend now, not a lover.

He looked closely at her sleeping face, realizing he could see little of Anna. They were sisters, but nothing like each other in *personality*. His feelings for Anna had never moved beyond friendship and a desire to protect. Molly was a different matter. Even with all his worries, he couldn't deny his desire for her. He kept his mind on the thorny problems before them, but at moments like this, when she was unaware of him, he studied her, testing the measure of his own feelings. That she was desirable went without saying. He could easily fantasize for hours about kissing her full lips, about letting his lips trace down her cheek and neck and...

Getting involved with Molly—or anyone else—was a ticket to hell, in his opinion. Once a person opened his heart to caring, he was setting himself up for pain. Thomas had seen it firsthand as a young boy and then again as a young man, when he'd fallen in love with Jessie West. That relationship had taught him the mathematical equation of love equals suffering.

He'd vowed never to care that much again, but his heart had pulled a fast one on him with Molly. He already cared—a lot. All those years working as a cowboy, alone and safe on the range, were for naught. The safety net of his computer work, where most of his colleagues were more involved with binary patterns and techno language than relationships, had failed to protect him from love. He'd known Molly for only a matter of hours, and already he was lost.

If he were the kind of man who ran away from danger, he'd be headed in the opposite direction; yet he could no more abandon Molly than he could fly to the moon.

He stopped his thoughts and focused on the road in front of him. The last thing they needed was to get pulled over by a state trooper for speeding. He had no doubt that Sheriff Johnson had alerted the entire southwest part of the country of his escape. Every lawman sporting a badge would be looking for him.

What he had to do was keep his mind on the task at hand. If his feelings for Molly were real, they would still be there when his name was cleared and Kate was found. For right now, he would just drive.

When the sun marked midmorning, he pulled over at a service station for gas and touched Molly's shoulder. Her eyelids fluttered and opened, her clear gaze on him like a caress. "Where are we?"

"We're almost there." He saw the tension leap back into her face, and he regretted what his words cost her.

"Want me to drive?" Molly asked.

"Okay." He handed her the keys. "Let's grab a bite and head for the motel where Darwin is staying."

Molly got a bag of burgers while Thomas gassed up the car. Familiar wasn't happy about his chicken fingers—a fact that made Thomas smile as he realized that he was attuned to the feline's gourmet tastes.

When they got back on the road, Familiar sat on his lap and tapped with his paw the location of the Tumbleweed Motel on the map Thomas had printed off the Internet.

"I think he's ready for a tête-à-tête with Darwin," Thomas said. "If Darwin knows anything about Kate, I'll bet Familiar can make him spill his guts."

"I hope so." Molly's face was grim. "I've

been thinking about the couple who camped near you." She kept her gaze on the road. "Do you remember their names?"

"John and Judy something. I don't think they ever said their last names, and they were gone before the cops could find them."

"I saw their camp location. They were pretty close to you."

"Right." He frowned, trying to follow her line of reasoning. "So?"

"They left before dawn. Doesn't that strike you as odd?"

It hadn't at the time, but now that he was really thinking about it, it *was* odd. Campers often packed up at daybreak, but few broke camp in the middle of the night. "Where are you going with this?"

"You said you grilled steaks or—"

"They grilled steaks. I actually had some fish I'd caught."

"Did you drink anything?"

"Judy made some coffee."

Molly slowed the car and pulled over. "You didn't hear anything when they took down their tent and loaded all their gear? Not the first sound?"

He shook his head. "I'm a pretty light sleeper, so I can't explain why I didn't hear them. I just remember waking with an awful headache."

"Is it possible Judy might have put something in your food or coffee?"

"To what purpose?"

"So that you wouldn't hear them leaving. Thomas, I've been thinking. What would make my sister hide in your bedroom closet? Why would your alibi pack up in the middle of the night? This John and Judy couple, if the sheriff had found them, could have said you were at the campsite all night. That would have completely cleared you of the suspicion of my sister's murder. But John and Judy were conveniently gone."

Thomas noticed that Familiar was watching Molly intently, his head nodding slightly as he listened, as if he were agreeing with what she was saying.

"Do you think this whole thing could be about me?" he asked.

"I'm not sure," she said slowly as she put the car back on the road. "But I don't have a doubt that you were a big part of the plan. Either as a scapegoat or because someone wanted to hurt you in a big time kind of way."

Thomas stroked Familiar's sleek back. "If I was drugged, we could test the coffee."

"When I went to the campsite, I saw some of your equipment there. Since it didn't figure into the murder, the police left it."

"It would help a lot if I could figure out when the frame began." He clenched his hands into fists. "They're always one step ahead of me."

"Let's hope Darwin isn't. I think we just made our destination."

Thomas looked out the front window at the rundown hotel they were approaching. They were on the outskirts of Brownsville, an area that looked as if it remained in the Great Depression. Grim was the only word he could think of to describe it.

Molly pulled into the parking lot, the sound of gravel crunching beneath the car tires. Her expression was tight and angry.

"Looks like Darwin is on the run." Thomas eased Familiar onto the seat.

"Not nearly as much as he's going to be," Molly said as she found a parking spot and stopped.

When she started to open the door, Thomas put a hand on her arm. "Molly, even if he confesses, no one will take our word for it. We need to tape record the conversation."

She put her hands on the steering wheel.

"You're right. Can we get the proper equipment?"

"We need to find an electronics store. The equipment isn't complicated." He looked at her. "I could wire you up and we'd be able to record everything."

Molly's lips turned up into a smile. "Thomas, you're a genius."

"I may be a fool," he said. "If this goes wrong, if he suspects you're wired, this could be really bad."

"He'll never suspect." She grasped his hands. "Thomas, I can pull this off. He'll never know."

"It isn't as easy as you think. Folks get nervous. It shows."

"I can do this." She took his hand and placed it against her chest. "Feel my heartbeat. Strong and steady. When I was in high school—" the determination on her face was replaced with sadness "—Anna wanted to be an actress. That's the only reason I tried out for the play. For her. She was too nervous."

"And you got the part," Thomas finished.

"I didn't even want it, but I did it. Anna worked backstage on the sets. Every night I'd look in the wings and see her watching. See the desire in her face." Molly looked down at her lap. "I feel like I cheated her out of things."

When she looked up again, her gaze was piercing and cold. "I can do this, Thomas. Let's get the equipment and then let me at him."

Forty minutes later they were back in the parking lot. Molly had taped the microphone to her chest with tape. The recorder was hooked inside the back of her pants. She put her hand on the car door.

"He might not even be there." Thomas had a bad feeling.

Molly picked up her cell phone and dialed the number for the motel. "Would you please connect me with Darwin Goodman's room?" she asked.

Thomas could hear the manager's voice but he couldn't discern what was being said. Molly held him with her gaze.

"I must have gotten his name wrong. Tall guy with a rose tattoo on his left arm. I borrowed some money from him last night and he told me to bring it to him here."

Thomas saw the satisfaction touch her face and knew she'd gotten what she wanted. His thought was confirmed when she looked at him and whispered. "He's ringing Darwin's room."

Her expression changed. "Hello, Darwin." Her voice was like a sharp blade. "It's Molly Harper, your sister-in-law. I need to talk to you, and don't bother trying to run away. I'm sitting outside your door."

She hung up the phone. "Hurry before he tries to take off."

"Remember, the recorder is voice activated," he said. "Whenever anyone talks or makes a sound, it'll start to record."

She got out of the car and hooked the wire into the recorder. She motioned for him to get behind the wheel. "I think it might be best if you moved the car around behind the hotel."

"Will you take Familiar?" he asked as he walked around the car.

She shook her head. "Darwin hates animals. If he sees Familiar, it'll only delay what I have to do while he rants."

"How will I know if you need me?" Thomas asked.

"I'll be fine. I promise." She kissed him lightly on the cheek and turned to walk away. Familiar darted toward the window, but Thomas caught him.

"We can't help her," he told the cat.

Molly's stride was long, her back straight

and commanding as she walked across the gritty parking lot.

Thomas took a seat behind the wheel. Beside him, Familiar growled softly.

"We have to trust her," Thomas said. "Like it or not, that's what we have to do."

# Chapter Nine

*Molly is a smart cookie and all of that, but I fear she's underestimating the people who killed her sister. I'm worried about her. Thomas is, too. Yet here we sit, waiting.*

*I learned a lot at the crime scene, and none of it makes me happy. Anna was in Thomas's bedroom. She hid in the closet while someone else was in the house. The way the scene plays out in my head is that the killer came into the bedroom, found her and either convinced or forced her out of the closet.*

*Anna knew where Thomas kept his gun and she tried to use it to defend herself. The end result was that the killer took the gun from her and used it to kill her. This has the sound of a robbery gone bad, except for a couple of things, the biggest of which is baby Kate's disappearance. A robber doesn't commit a murder, leave anything of value* and steal a baby. If the killing was unanticipated, why didn't the killer just leave the baby?

So the next big question is—what was Anna involved in? She took the baby away from her home, and I have to believe she knew she was in danger. She protected Kate, because she felt the baby was in a dangerous position, too. Dangerous because of Darwin, because of Anna, or because of Kate's real father? If we don't figure out what Anna was up to, we may never find Kate.

We do know that Anna was far more complex than anyone thought. She had a lover, a man she never mentioned to anyone. Could she have taken Kate to her father? Then why did the person who sent Molly the note sound so urgent, as if Kate were in danger?

This is one of the most puzzling cases I've ever worked. There's so much at stake— Thomas's freedom and the life of a baby. It's just amazing to me how humanoids do things that make life so much more complicated than it needs to be. Why didn't Anna just leave Darwin if she didn't love him? Why stay with a man who brutalized her? Why not tell her sister and family what was *happening in her life? I could write a book on the foibles of the biped. When I retire, I just might do that.*

*Now I need to comfort Thomas. He's about to come apart at the seams. The hardest thing for a man like him to do is to sit back and wait. I'll give him a rub under his chin and a sandpaper tongue on his cheek. While I'm at it I need to convey to him that we need a change of menu. I've eaten my last bite of fast food.*

*Ah, he's relaxing and stroking my back. I can feel his blood pressure beginning to drop. We'll be chilled and ready when Molly needs us, which could be any minute now.*

MOLLY FORCED HER WAY into the motel room when Darwin cracked open the door. Her nerve faltered. As long as she'd been beside Thomas, she'd felt strong, but standing in the doorway of the room, alone with Darwin, she wasn't so certain she could force him to talk.

He looked wild; his hair was unkempt; he hadn't shaved and wore unironed clothes—and Darwin was nothing if not vain. Even as she thought it, she saw his hand move up to push the dirty strands off his forehead. He was a handsome man, swarthy, and proud of his good looks. A real bad boy. Grunge was not his modus oper-andi.

"How the hell did you find me?" Darwin demanded. He glanced beyond her at the parking lot. "I covered my tracks. Did you come by yourself?"

"I'm here to ask you questions." She forced steel into her voice. "And you'd better answer."

"Or what?"

"Don't mess with me, Darwin. My sister is dead and my niece is missing."

"There's nothing I can do about it." His gaze shifted beyond her to the parking lot again. "Come in if you're coming, or better yet, just leave. I don't have anything to say to you."

Molly stepped into the room, aware that the bed was unmade and dirty clothes were thrown all over the floor. Her panic rose as Darwin closed the door behind her and locked it. As soon as that was done, Darwin walked past her and went to the window, looking out at the parking lot again. He was so nervous he radiated energy.

"What are you so afraid of?" she asked, deliberately speaking in a calm tone.

"Someone's trying to kill me," he said. "That's what I'm afraid of—dying."

Of all the answers Darwin might have

given, that was one she hadn't anticipated. "Someone's trying to kill *you?*" She'd suspected Darwin of running off because of his misdeeds, not to save his skin.

He gave her a contemptuous look. "I forget there's something wrong with the hearing of you Harper women. That's what I said. Someone has been trying to kill me ever since the night Anna was murdered. So, beat it so I can save my hide."

Darwin was still the charmer Molly remembered, always worried about himself and no one else. "I heard you—I just find it hard to believe. What happened, all those chickens come home to roost? You cheated someone out of something, didn't you?"

Darwin glared at her, but he didn't move from the window. "Believe what you want to, but that sister of yours was far from a saint."

Molly felt her temper start to climb. "How dare you!" She walked to him, right up to his face. "How dare you talk about Anna like that? She gave up so many things for you!"

"What movie have you been watching?" Darwin asked as he sneered. "Your sister didn't give up anything at all."

"Except her physical safety and her relationship with her family. You hit her and she was so ashamed she couldn't tell me the truth."

Darwin gave Molly a scathing look. "She needed a lot worse than what I gave her."

Molly felt a rush of fury so strong she felt her body begin to shake. She had to control herself. Trading insults with Darwin wasn't going to do a bit of good. She had to be smarter than him, to trick him into telling her where Kate was.

"I came here for one reason. What happened to Katie?" she asked, fighting to keep her voice level.

"How should I know?"

"You have to know. Where is she?"

"If I did know, I wouldn't tell you." He dropped the curtain and went to his suitcase on the bed. Picking up clothes from the floor, he started packing. "I'm getting out of here. If you found me, they will, too."

"Who will?"

He slammed the suitcase shut. "You're probably too hardheaded to take any advice, but I'll give it to you nonetheless. Get out of here and get out fast. The folks who're after me don't care whether you're male or female. They'll hurt you."

He picked up the suitcase and started toward the door.

"I can't let you leave." Molly stepped in front of him, barring his way.

"Woman, get out of my way or I'll do what I have to do to get out of here."

"Tell me where Katie is. That's all I want to know."

"I told you, I don't know. Anna left the house with her about seven o'clock that night. Anna said she was going over to Rachel's, but when I checked, she'd never been there. Rachel hadn't seen Anna or the baby. That was the last time I saw my wife or my baby girl, when they were walking out the door. And you might keep in mind that Anna left with a lie on her lips."

It wasn't emotion in Darwin's voice that caught Molly's attention, but the fact that he called Kate his baby girl.

"Have you even bothered to look for the baby?"

Darwin's eyes narrowed. "Let me tell you something about your precious Anna. From the day Katie was born, Anna acted like I had nothing to do with her. She never let me hold that baby or feed her or change her diaper. It was Anna and Kate, and I wasn't part of that happy little family. She made that very clear. Once she had Kate, she didn't need me anymore. Now Kate is gone. They say she's dead."

He reached beside Molly and grasped the doorknob. "Now you get out of my way. I'm not going to sit here and wait for those men to come and kill me."

"Did you kill Anna?" Molly asked, leaning her full weight against the door.

"Are you insane? Why would I kill my wife?"

"Who did kill Anna?"

Darwin's eyes shifted to the door and back. "Keep hanging around here and you'll find out, but it won't do you any good. You'll be dead, too."

"Where'd you get the money in your bank account, Darwin? Did you sell Katie?"

His eyes narrowed. "Poking your nose around is going to get you killed, just like it got Anna killed. The men who killed Anna don't mess around. They'll kill you and me and anyone who threatens their deal. They paid me money to disappear, and that's what I intend to do. I'm headed for Mexico or some place farther south. Now move out of my way!"

He pulled at the door, but Molly refused to budge. "Was Anna seeing another man?"

Darwin let go of the door to look at her. "Anna wasn't stupid. She'd never cheat on me."

Molly had her answer. Darwin never suspected that Kate wasn't his, not even with the way Anna had treated him. "Who were Anna's friends? Who is this Rachel?"

He shrugged. "After Kate was born, Anna started jogging to lose the fat from the pregnancy. She made friends with a bunch of those health nuts. They went jogging all over the place, up to the parks, everywhere. She took Kate in a stroller. She was obsessed with getting fit."

"What are some names?"

"Mostly a bunch of women, but a couple of scrawny guys. I don't recall any names."

"Who is Rachel?" Molly wanted to strangle Darwin. He had so little interest in Anna that he hadn't even bothered to learn the names of her friends.

"Rachel Alain, a big lawyer's wife. Another health freak and do-gooder."

Molly decided to try another tack. "If Anna left with Kate, maybe she took the baby someplace safe. Who did she trust?"

A look of comprehension slipped into Darwin's eyes. "There was a—"

Molly felt her body jolt. She stumbled

away from the door as it flew open. Before she could turn around, something hard crashed into her head. As she fell to the floor, she heard the sound of a gunshot, and then everything was silent.

THOMAS HIT THE BUTTONS on the radio and listened to the newscast from Dallas. His jailbreak wasn't the big story it had been two days before. Not even a mention on the radio. That news should have lessened his tension, but he kept glancing at his watch.

Familiar was acting weird. The cat, who was normally so well behaved, had tried to sharpen his claws on the car seat. Now the handsome black feline was pacing back and forth across the dash, pawing at the window. Certainly he wanted out of the car, but Thomas had promised Molly he'd keep Familiar safe in the vehicle.

Molly had been gone half an hour. Thomas was getting worried; Darwin wasn't much of a talker, so what could they be doing for half an hour? The images that flashed through his mind weren't pleasant.

"Meow!" Familiar leaped to the seat and dug both front paws into Thomas's legs.

"Hey!" Thomas said, unhooking the cat

and putting him on the seat. "She told us to wait, but I agree with you. We should go."

"Meow!" Familiar cried, hurtling against the car door.

Thomas opened the door. "We'll go check on her even if she gets angry. Darwin will be shocked to see me, but if he gets out of hand, just jump on his head and I'll clock him."

The cat bolted out of the car and darted down the pavement. Thomas was right on his heels.

As soon as he saw the door of the motel room standing open, Thomas knew something bad had come down. Familiar ran into the room, but Thomas paused, listening. It was one thing for a cat to dart into a room, but another for a man. If Darwin was holding a gun on Molly, he might be spooked into using it.

The curtains on the window were pulled tight, and though he tried to see into the room, it was futile. He listened, hoping to get a hint of what was happening. The only thing he heard was silence, until Familiar gave a yowl of distress.

Thomas couldn't wait any longer. He kicked the door wide and rushed into the room, looking for someone to slug.

The room appeared empty, until his eyes

adjusted to the dimness. He saw the furniture had been scrambled, as if a fight had taken place.

Clothes were scattered across the floor, and there was a suitcase on the bed. He switched on the overhead light. The scene that was revealed was something from one of his worst nightmares.

Molly lay sprawled on the floor beside the bed, a black pool of blood beside her head. His heart lurched into his stomach.

"Molly!" He knelt beside her and felt for a pulse. To his relief, her heartbeat was strong. Her skin was warm, and though her breathing was a little shallow, she wasn't in distress.

It wasn't until he'd made sure Molly was alive that he noticed the gun in her right hand. He removed it.

"Where did this come from?" he asked Familiar, who stood beside Molly, a paw on her cheek. The cat looked at Thomas and moved to the other side of the bed. Familiar waited, as if he expected Thomas to follow him.

The bad feeling from earlier grew stronger. Thomas followed the cat. When he was halfway around the bed, he stopped. Darwin Goodman lay on the floor, a gunshot wound to his heart. His eyes were open and glazed, and Thomas knew he was dead.

It registered on Thomas that this was exactly the same scenario as Anna's murder. Someone had come in, killed Darwin, and planted the gun on Molly.

He hurried back to her. "Molly, wake up." He got a wet cloth from the bathroom and bathed her face. She'd been smacked on the head, and he couldn't tell how severe it was. "Wake up, Molly." He knew it wouldn't be long before someone reported the gunshot and the police would be on them. If she didn't come to soon, he'd scoop her up and take her to a hospital.

Familiar joined him in working to revive Molly. The cat licked her face, and slowly her eyelids fluttered up. She moaned and started to touch her head.

"What happened?" she asked

"Don't try to move." He wiped her forehead with the cool cloth. "You were struck on the head."

"From behind, the weasel." Molly lifted one leg and then the other. She shifted her body. "Everything seems to work okay. I guess Darwin took the golden opportunity to cut and run."

Thomas hesitated. "Not exactly."

"Help me sit up."

Thomas gave her his hand and pulled her into a sitting position. "Before you try to stand, let me look at your head." A big knot had already begun to form, but the actual wound in her scalp wasn't too bad. "It would heal better if you got a couple of stitches."

"Forget it. We can't afford the publicity. Help me up. We have to get on Darwin's trail. He knows more than he's saying. The fool acted like someone was trying to kill him."

Thomas held her steady as she gained her feet. She was a little woozy, but she got her balance quickly. "Molly, did you see the person who struck you?"

"No. But I heard something. A gunshot?" She looked at him, her expression changing from curiosity to concern. "Where's Darwin?"

"He's dead." Thomas nodded to the other side of the bed. "Someone shot him in the heart. Then they put the gun in your hand." He pointed to the gun on the floor.

"What are we going to do?"

Before Thomas could answer they heard the sound of sirens.

# *Chapter Ten*

*In the parlance of the old cowboys, We'd better head for the hills. Molly is still a bit unsteady, but Thomas has her in his capable arms. I've checked the parking lot, and there's a trail back through some scrub and a dry creek bed where we can hide out for the moment.*

*Thomas has the gun in his hand, so we won't leave Molly's fingerprints behind, but there's no time to check and see if we're leaving any other evidence. She could have touched anything in the room, and once those forensic guys dust the place, the law will know she was here. I knew when I got the call to help Molly that there was the possibility of trouble with the police. What I didn't realize was that I'd be on the run from justice with two potential murder suspects, one of whom is an escapee. I'm on the wrong side of Texas law enforcement.*

*Thomas has the good sense to follow me, and I'm making tracks as fast as my little black kitty paws will allow. At last we're in the cover of the scrub trees. Places in Texas are quite lush, but this part of the state isn't blessed with a lot of shrubbery. Everything might be bigger in this state, but not the foliage.*

*Molly is looking a little green around the gills. All of this running isn't good with a head wound, but Thomas has her tight against him. His expression tells me that he's fallen hard for her, even if he doesn't know it himself. Molly is harder to read, which is interesting. Women are usually more open about their feelings, but not Molly. She's sewed up tight. I'd love to hear the story behind her. And I'm sure Thomas would be all ears.*

*Now, though, we're heading down the creek bed. I've calculated how far we have to go to get to the car. I'm glad Thomas parked far enough away to give us a chance at escape.*

*Darwin's murder is only going to re-ignite the search for Thomas. The law will conclude—and not without good reason—that Thomas escaped and, with Molly's help, killed Darwin. If they catch us near the scene of the murder, nothing will ever make them search for another killer. They'll pop*

*Thomas in jail for Anna's murder and Darwin's murder, and Molly will go with him as an accomplice. If we're nabbed here at the scene, I see nothing but trouble with a capital T.*

*I'm going to climb what passes for a tree here in South Texas and see if I can gain a vantage point. I don't know what genus this poor thing belongs to, but I'm going up it. I'm just high enough to see the police pull into the parking lot of the motel. Five squad cars, so they aren't taking any chances. They're moving to the door, guns at the ready. Now's our chance to make a break for the car. If we can slip through that open space, we'll be just fine.*

*Molly is leaning heavily on Thomas, but he acts like she doesn't weigh more than a feather. It's either desperation or love, and I vote for the second.*

*One, two, three…go! We made it to the car, and Thomas has Molly in the passenger seat. Now he's behind the wheel. He's taking it slow and steady, so as not to draw attention. As one of my favorite Texans, Willie Nelson, would sing—"On the road again."*

MOLLY PASTED a blank expression on her face, determined not to give away how much her head hurt. Thomas had been attacked and whacked in the head back in Jefferson, and now someone had hit her from behind. Thomas had been stoic about it, and she was determined to do no less, even if her head throbbed so hard it made her vision blur. A bit of pain wasn't important. Darwin Goodman was dead, and though she'd never liked him, she was still shocked by his brutal murder. She'd also pinned a lot of hope on Darwin being able to help her find Kate. She'd believed that somehow he knew where the baby was. She'd pinned her hopes on it, and now she felt despondency gnawing at her. It seemed that instead of getting closer, Kate was slipping away.

The one thing she'd gleaned was more a gut feeling than a fact—Darwin wasn't involved in Anna's murder or Kate's disappearance. Not actively involved. Anna's husband had been a swaggering piece of work, but no one deserved to be murdered. Not even Darwin.

She was drawn from her thoughts by the worried looks Thomas kept casting at her.

"Molly, let me find a doctor for you," he said.

Since they'd left the city streets behind,

Thomas was driving fast. The speedometer needle hovered close to a hundred.

"I'm fine. Don't worry about me—focus on your driving. I'm in a lot more danger from a wreck than a knock on the head."

"You don't look fine."

She smiled. She couldn't help it. His concern touched her. "I have a headache, which is only natural. How long do you think I was unconscious?"

After a pause, he said, "How long did you talk to Darwin?"

She shook her head, then gave a small cry. Thomas hit the brakes and pulled into the parking lot of a flea market. "What is it?"

"The tape! I forgot all about it, but the tape should have picked up what the killers said." She glanced behind them. The road was empty. They could afford a moment without drawing undue attention to themselves.

"You're right! I was so worried that Darwin would find out you were wired. It never occurred to me to worry that the real killers would show up."

"Me, neither." She sighed. "I didn't ask the right questions, Thomas. I wasted our chance. When you hear the tape, you'll see."

He touched her face, gently turning her

head so that she looked at him. "I'm sure that isn't true, but you have to remember, Molly, we aren't criminals. Maybe we don't know the right questions to ask because it isn't in our nature to commit criminal acts."

"Now Darwin's dead, and if he knew anything, we'll never find out." She felt a lump in her throat that made it hard to talk. On top of everything else, she wasn't going to cry in front of Thomas again. "Damn it. I just want to find Kate and then find the people who killed Anna. That's what Sheriff Johnson should be doing, but he isn't."

"Give me the recorder," Thomas requested.

She removed it from her waistband and worked the wire up through her shirt. When she handed it to him, his hand closed over hers, holding tightly for a moment.

"Let's get somewhere safe and listen to it."

"I don't know anywhere that would be safe. Play it now, please," she answered. The landscape was empty. They had no friends in the area, no one to turn to. The police would be narrowing the net around them. Eventually, she knew, they would be caught. If they didn't find answers soon, it would be too late for them.

Thomas glanced in the rearview mirror at a car rapidly approaching them. He put the car in drive and hit the gas hard, pulling out and away. "We can't do this on the side of a road. The law will have a dragnet out in a matter of hours. We need to get away from this area before we get caught in the search for Darwin's killers. We'll find a motel and check in." Thomas put the tape in his pocket and clenched the steering wheel with both hands. "Once we have a place to stop, we'll have a listen to the tape. Just pray there's something useful on it."

Familiar turned in a circle on the front seat. He walked over to Molly. "Meow!" He tapped her stomach in an insistent manner.

"First we need to find some grub for our feline friend," Thomas said. "Something fresh and from the Gulf, I'd say. I realize dining out isn't a high priority, but I think we should treat ourselves to a good meal tonight. I think if we don't, Familiar is going to quit the case."

Molly put her hand on his thigh and gave it a squeeze. He was doing everything in his power to help her. How long had it been since she'd felt someone else was truly on her side? She couldn't remember.

"Look! There's a place up ahead." She

pointed to a quaint-looking building that appeared as they climbed a slight rise. "The sign says the Boone Docks." She smiled at Thomas. "It looks a little peculiar, but why not? I'd give a lot for a hot bath."

"Why not indeed?" Thomas whipped the car into the parking lot, driving around the old two-story house made of logs until he found a secluded parking spot in the shade. "Maybe they'll have a room."

Molly and Familiar got out. She walked toward a pecan tree ringed with daffodils. Long ago, when she was a small girl, she'd frequently visited her grandmother. Time had erased so many of the details of Grams, but one came back strong, and that was the flower beds. Grams had had a way with bulbs, and her yard had been a riot of daffodils, paper whites, tulips, and hyacinths.

Kneeling, Molly touched one of the beautiful yellow flowers. At her home in Phoenix she had flowers. But would she ever see her home again?

When she stood up, Thomas was watching her from the front porch of the hotel. He beckoned her toward him.

"They have one room left, and Miss Lily is putting supper on the table now. She was so charmed by Familiar that she's going to broil some fresh trout for him."

Molly picked up the cat. "I've been so caught up in things I haven't taken care of Familiar the way I should have. I wouldn't say food is my highest priority, but I have to admit, I'm starving. I can't remember the last time we ate."

Thomas stepped closer to her. "We could look for another place if you aren't comfortable with the arrangement."

"No, it's fine." She and Thomas had shared close quarters before. One room wouldn't be a problem. Even as she thought it, she felt she was lying to herself. As she followed him inside, she had the sense she'd stepped across an invisible line. Because of Thomas, her life was changed in ways that weren't fully clear to her yet. All she knew was that she felt a rush of joy when their gazes locked.

Thomas held the door and she entered in front of him. Just inside, she stopped. The Boone Docks was a step back to frontier time. The interior walls were the same chinked logs as the exterior. A fire burned in a fireplace large enough to roast an ox where a black pot bubbled and the aroma of something delicious came to her.

"Feels like ol' Dan'l should step through the door, doesn't it?" Thomas asked.

"Except for the modern lighting, this could be the 1800s." Molly turned slowly around.

"This hotel dates back to 1792," a sprightly voice said from behind the counter.

Molly turned to face the elderly woman who smiled at her. "You're Miss Lily?"

"None other, and you must be Mrs. Smith." She gave Molly a look that let her know she was nobody's fool. "Your Mr. Smith has charmed me into giving up my last room. The man has a way with words and some of the best manners I've seen in the past fifty years."

Molly felt a blush creeping up her cheeks. Thomas had undoubtedly felt that lying about their marital status was preferable to offending the sensibilities of Miss Lily. No matter, since the hotel keeper was onto the fake name he'd selected. Smith. What a giveaway!

"My, uh, husband is a very charming man," Molly managed to say without laughing.

"I'll have Alfred retrieve your bags and take them to your room." Miss Lily turned the old-fashioned registration ledger toward Molly.

"Mr. and Mrs. John Smith." Molly read aloud and rolled her eyes at Thomas. "How original, darling."

"Is something wrong?" Miss Lily asked, her eyebrows arched.

"Mo...my wife is just tired." Thomas took Molly's arm, as if to assist her. His grip was firm, cautioning her not to give them away. "We're both tired. If we could just have the key to our room."

"Before you do anything else, you must eat." Miss Lily picked up Familiar. "This cat is ravenous. I can tell. I've had a lot of experience with hungry kitties."

Thomas stepped forward and smiled. "It's so good of you to cater to the cat. Perhaps Familiar would like to eat now, but I think my wife and I would like to rest for a bit."

Molly knew the only thing he wanted was to get to the room and listen to the tape, but she could tell Miss Lily was not going to be thwarted.

"You'll rest better with some food in your stomach." Miss Lily was firm. "Your wife looks like she's about to fall over."

"Meow!" Familiar put a paw on Miss Lily's face and then licked her, distracting her.

"Oh, this boy's a true delight, isn't he? Our

hotel cat died last year, and I've missed having a feline around the place." Miss Lily glanced from Thomas to Familiar. "This one seems particularly bright."

"Unbelievably," Thomas said. "Could we have room service?"

"I'm sorry, but the Boone Docks is designed to be more communal, like the old inns that used to dot the stage trails." Miss Lily looked over her glasses at Thomas and then Molly. "It's a good thing you've settled here for the night. There was a murder at a motel about twenty miles from here. Police are looking for an escaped prisoner, from over near the Louisiana line."

"Imagine that." Molly kept her gaze from sliding. How much did Miss Lily know, and what did she intend to do with her knowledge?

"There aren't any televisions in the hotel rooms, but there's one down here in the front parlor. Our guests sometimes come down for a social hour. I serve brandy, port and sherry, and those that have the itch watch a bit of television."

"That sounds nice," Molly said.

"I don't hold much with television." Miss Lily's gaze was clear and direct. "Lots of misinformation. I mean folks like you, traveling with a cat and all, I'll bet you don't much care for the boob tube, either?"

"Not in the least. Where's the dining room?" It was going to be simpler to comply with Miss Lily's game plan than to resist her. The one thing Molly didn't want to do was put Miss Lily on the alert.

"I'll show you," the hotel keeper said, leading them down a dark hallway toward the sounds of cutlery and laughter. "There's a nice table here with a view of the garden."

Thirty minutes later Thomas sighed with contentment. "The food is better than I imagined. I hate to admit it, but Miss Lily was right. We needed some nutrition." He pointed at the cat, who'd curled up on his chair and fallen into a sound sleep.

"I could sleep for a week, but that isn't an option, is it?" Molly had managed to eat, but her stomach was tight with anxiety. With each passing hour, it seemed she was more firmly caught in the web of Anna's murder and Kate's disappearance. No one in the dining room had given them a second glance, but after the evening news, they might be recognized.

"I think we can safely retire to our room

without drawing suspicion or offending Miss Lily and her cook," Thomas said.

Molly rose, picking Familiar up in her arms. "Let's do it," she said.

She was almost across the dining room when the cell phone in her purse began to ring. With Thomas watching, she answered.

"You must find that baby. If you ever want to see her again, find her quickly."

The line went dead. Molly turned to Thomas, the phone slipping from her hand.

Thomas picked up the cell phone from the floor, slid it into his pocket and took Molly's elbow. In a matter of moments she was out of the dining room, down the hall and into the safety of the room, where she told him what had just happened.

THOMAS HAD CONVINCED Molly to hold off on listening to the tape until he brought her a glass of brandy. The phone call had shaken her to her very toes. He'd spent the past ten minutes calming her enough so that he was comfortable to leave her alone in the room.

He hurried down the hallway, darting quickly back into the room when he heard the sound of voices approaching. Miss Lily's gossip about the television had unnerved him. Already he was connected with the murder of Darwin Goodman. If Molly's prints were found, it wouldn't be long before she was implicated, too. The best course of action was to remain as out-of-sight as possible on the off chance someone might recognize him from a television report.

The silence in the room was thick. "Molly?" he whispered softly. She was pretty much a nervous wreck, and if she'd fallen asleep, he certainly didn't want to wake her.

"I want to play the tape," she said.

Her voice sounded lifeless, as if she'd suppressed all emotion in an effort not to crumble. That worried Thomas more than anything else. And it brought back some harsh memories that made his own heart turn chill. His own mother had sounded like that after the death of his sister. When Amber had been killed by a hit-and-run driver, his mother had simply given up. She'd died inch by inch. And he'd been forced to watch it, unable to help or change anything. He'd only been fifteen, too young to help his mom recover from the tragic death and too old to hide from what was happening.

"We'll find Kate." He handed her the glass

of brandy. Her hand was cold when it brushed his.

"In time?"

From her seat by the window Molly looked at him, as if he might say the magic words that would save her. As much as Thomas wanted to give her the comfort she so desperately needed, he couldn't lie to her. "We'll do our best. That's all we can do." He picked up the recorder.

"Do you think Kate's in imminent danger?"

"No." That wasn't a lie. "I think the danger has to do with movement. I believe the caller was warning that the people who have Kate are planning to move her."

"Because they know she's stolen?"

He shook his head. "I don't know. But I don't think Kate is in physical danger. I think we're in danger of losing her trail if we don't act quickly."

"I don't think Darwin said anything that can really help us find Kate, but maybe you'll hear it differently."

He pressed the play button. The first words were Darwin's, demanding to know what she was doing there and who had followed her.

Thomas listened to the exchange between Molly and her brother-in-law with growing anxiety. Darwin did sound afraid. And rightly so, as it turned out. But Darwin had to have known why he was being hunted down. Molly hadn't been able to elicit that information from him.

There was the sound of someone forcing entry into the room, and the whump of Molly's body hitting the floor.

"Look, man, please don't kill me. I'll—" Darwin never got a chance to finish his sentence. The gunshot rang out in the small motel room.

Molly flinched, and Thomas put his arms around her. As he held her, they listened to the rest of the tape.

"What are we going to do about her?" a masculine voice asked.

"Shut up and let me think," a second male voice answered.

Thomas had no doubt he was referring to Molly. They were talking about killing her as if she were nothing.

"We should have killed the baby, too. I told you no loose ends. Now look! She's hunting that kid." The first man was speaking again. "Let's kill her and move on."

"Shut up, I said." There was a pause before the second man spoke again. "Put the gun in her hand and let's get out of here."

The tape ended.

When Molly turned to Thomas, he saw the hope in her eyes.

"We have evidence that I didn't kill Darwin. We can mail the tape to the police."

He wanted to encourage her hope, because it was the first hint of life he'd seen in her since the phone call. But he couldn't lie.

"There's no way to prove where the tape was made, or when," he said. "I'm sorry, but it doesn't help us at all."

"Except that I'm positive Kate is alive." She rose and began to pace the room. "And that's something. That's a lot. Now we just have to work harder to find her."

Thomas felt such a sense of relief that he didn't say anything. Molly had found her strength again. She wasn't going to quit. She was going to find her niece.

"Is something wrong?" Molly asked. "You're sure looking at me funny."

Thomas walked to her and put his hands on her shoulders. He held her gently as he stared into her eyes. "Nothing is wrong. I just realized something about myself."

"What's that?" she asked.

"That I've let the past shape everything about my life."

She didn't understand. He could see it in the puzzled look in her eyes.

"My dad died when I was young, and my mother died when I was a teenager. She died of grief. She just stopped wanting to live. The first woman I fell in love with was afraid to love me back."

"I'm sorry, Thomas."

He shook his head, touching her lips like a whisper. "It's okay. I've been sorry all my life. Sorry that I couldn't change things for my mom, sorry that love hurt so much. I lost my sister, my mom and dad and Jessie. Somehow, I believed that if I loved anyone again, they would leave me, too."

He saw the compassion in her eyes, but she was wise enough to remain silent and let him talk.

"I think back on the first few times Anna visited. I think she may have wanted more than friendship. But that's all I could offer her, all I ever offered anyone. Because I couldn't risk anything more."

Her hand touched his cheek, the most tender of touches, and he thought his heart would stop. "I'm telling you this, Molly, because, despite my best efforts, I've begun to love you."

# *Chapter Eleven*

Molly surrendered to Thomas's kiss. She had not planned for this moment, when he would once again draw her into his arms and kiss her, but she knew she wanted it. Needed it. And she gave herself to him with total abandon.

His confessions of doubt had touched her deeply—because she had her own secrets. And plenty of doubt, about herself and her past choices. Now wasn't the time to tell him, though. This moment was too precious to ruin with intrusions from her past. Now was only for Thomas. For the undeniable feelings they shared. In the darkness of a cold February night in Texas, Molly no longer cared to hold back her feelings.

She returned his kiss with a passion that flamed through her, burning hotly because it had been banked for so long. Now, though, she wasn't able to check her emotions.

She tore at the buttons of his shirt, not caring about anything but the feel of his skin against her. His fingers slipped beneath her shirt, pulling it over her head.

In a few seconds they were naked, their bodies entwined in a kiss. Thomas lifted her onto the bed, his lips never relinquishing their claim on hers.

The moonlight filtered in through the sheer curtains of the room, gilding his body in a soft glow. He was lean in the way of a cowboy, his body filled with a wiry strength. Molly thought he was the most handsome man she'd ever seen.

As they made love, greedily at first, then slowing, learning each other's desires and pleasures, Molly felt as if something deep inside of her had snapped. Some invisible restraint had broken, and she knew that she would be forever changed by this night and Thomas Lakeman.

*IT'S A DANG GOOD THING the windows in this old hotel open. The one by the bed is cracked, and with a bit of finagling, I've been able to enlarge the opening enough to slip through.*

*I'm glad Molly and Mr. Cowpoke have found the meaning of love, but I'm not into voyeurism. I think I'll take a jaunt around the hotel, burn off a few calories and see what's what.*

This bout of lovemaking was inevitable with the sparks flying between the two. Their restraint has been admirable, from a biped point of view. Felines are far more instinctual. We feel an urge, we act on it. Of course, we aren't big on recriminations, guilt, pride, remorse and the other things on the list of humanoid stumbling blocks. We make mistakes, but not like the bipeds.

In my line of work, I see a lot of misguided human emotions. Of course, I've met some of the finest people walking around, too. And some of the most villainous. I'm here to tell you, some humans can be downright vicious.

I'm not sorry that Darwin Goodman is dead. I'd be a hypocrite if I pretended I was. I hate it that Molly is afraid she may take the fall for the murder, but I'd never let that happen. So far, not a single one of my clients has gone to prison for a crime they didn't commit! The real rub here is that when Darwin died, he took what he knew about Kate with him. Based on what I heard on the tape, Darwin had no clue that Kate isn't his daughter. Yet he didn't seem overly worried *about her. That tells me that he knew what happened to her and felt she was safe enough. But how does that equate? What does "safe enough" mean to a man like Darwin?*

*There are a couple of things about Molly's cell phone call that bear looking into. Private phone numbers and cell phone numbers generally aren't published. So how did this mysterious caller get Molly's number? This indicates to me that someone in law enforcement could be involved. Lawmen are the only people with enough clout to get a cell number. It would be fairly easy for someone with a badge. And why not just tell Molly where Kate is? Why these cryptic messages, unless the caller has something to lose?*

*The other possibility is that the caller could have been someone with a background in subversive computer work. Maybe one of Thomas's and Anna's co-workers. Maybe even Lou Dial. Now that's a terrifying thought. I never suspected Lou. I've fallen down on the job. Time to rectify that!*

*Our leads in this part of Texas have come to an end with the death of Darwin. I think we need to pack up and head back to Jefferson. That may be the one place the cops don't expect to find us, and it's going to be where we find the answers to a lot of questions.*

*I'll have a word with Molly and Thomas about this when they finish up their personal business. And while I'm out prowling around, I think I'll check out the kitchen and see if any of that trout is left. I ate as much as I could, but all of this fretting and exercise have renewed my appetite, and who knows when I'll get the chance to eat again. Molly is a great gal, but regular feeding isn't at the top of her priority list.*

*Once the two lovers have settled down, I'll sneak back in the room and catch a little shut-eye. I intend to wake the two of them up at first light. We need to get going, and fast.*

*Hmm, the kitchen is empty, but the refrigerator is easy enough to open. There's my fish! I'll drag the plate out and snack down. I wish I could get it into the microwave, but that's too tall an order even for me. I'll settle for a cold buffet.*

*This isn't bad. I only wanted a taste, and now I think I'll scope out the rest of the hotel. There are those people who think the past is sacrosanct—nothing modern should intrude. I'm happy to say that such is not the case with the Boone Docks. While the past is cer-*

*tainly a large part of the hotel, modern conveniences such as toilets and refrigeration are included. It's certainly an interesting place, and Miss Lily is a force to be reckoned with. I doubt that she yields to many people. I have to say, I respect that. She's something else—probably a cat in a past life!*

*But hold on a minute. I'm passing the front parlor, and I hear the television. Big news story. Darwin's murder has been linked to Thomas's escape, but so far Molly isn't mentioned. I'll just slip up to the door and see if the newscaster is flashing a photo of Thomas. Yikes! There he is—big as life. And he looks just like himself. While Molly obviously finds him a handsome guy, I'd just as soon that his likeness wasn't spread across the news channels of Texas. It's only going to make it harder for us to investigate this case.*

*In the morning when we check out, I'm going to insist that Thomas take the bags and go to the car. His mug is just too recognizable.*

*Enough time has passed, I'm going to saunter back to the room and see if I can't catch some sleep. Felines normally require up to eighteen hours a day. So far, on this case, I'm averaging about six. Total. I need some shut-eye if I'm going to be at my best.*

THE TEXAS MOON fell across the bed, illuminating Molly in a light that was totally exotic. Thomas drank in the sight of her, reveling in her perfection. She was the most beautiful woman he'd ever seen. And she'd completely broken the protective barriers he'd kept around his heart.

A smart man would hitch a ride out of town and keep going as far as he could. Thomas had always considered himself smart, but Molly had slipped beneath his considerable defenses. She was extraordinary.

He moved from the bed to the chair beside the window where he could better watch her. When he'd worked as a cowboy, he'd spent nights on the range, watching the cattle graze and sleep. He'd felt more at home there than he had any other place, until tonight. While he'd learned how vulnerable he was where Molly was concerned, he'd also discovered how strong he could be—*for* her.

He knew so little about her, yet it didn't matter. Fate had thrown them together with a bond stronger than lust or love. Their very futures depended on each other. If their trust failed, they could both end up spending most of their lives in prison.

Molly turned in her sleep, a small cry

slipping from her lips. He felt the strongest urge to go to her and hold her, to protect her even from her dreams. He held himself back, though. One thing about Molly was that she brooked no interference. She would do what she had to, and neither Thomas nor anyone else would be allowed to interfere.

Even though he could stare at and think about Molly all night, Thomas forced his thoughts to the things that had occurred. He was worried about the phone call. Not many people could break into the records of a telephone company. The first thing that came to mind was law enforcement. With a search warrant, Sheriff Johnson could obtain almost any records he chose to ask for. That was par for the course. Thomas had checked the caller list and hadn't been surprised to find "unknown caller," which could mean the call had originated from an unrecognized area, or that someone had blocked his or her number.

What troubled Thomas more was the possibility that someone he viewed as a friend had dug up Molly's phone number and given it to—whom? Was that how he'd gotten set up as the fall guy for Anna's murder, by one of his co-workers?

Several of his buddies had the know-how

to find cell phone numbers, but why would they? And who was the woman who called? He could trace the call if he had the right equipment. But why would the woman who called urge Molly to find the baby if the folks who'd stolen Kate in the first place were behind killing Anna?

It was a circular puzzle without an answer. Thomas rose and quietly paced the room. None of it made sense, especially the fact that somehow, someone was keeping track of their every move. It was almost as if there was a tracking device in the car, but that was impossible. The car was a new rental. So how was someone tracing their movements?

All Thomas had were questions and precious few answers. When the sun broke the horizon, they would have to move on. Miss Lily made him nervous. She was elderly but sharp-eyed. She didn't miss much, and he was reasonably sure she suspected him and Molly already.

Though he knew he should sleep while he had the chance, he couldn't. Familiar had slipped out. Thomas glanced outside for the cat. Familiar would return in due time, of that he had no doubt. The cat was incredible.

Almost as if the cat had materialized because of his thoughts, Familiar slipped through the window. He gave Thomas a long stare, then curled up on the foot of the bed.

Thomas eased beneath the covers, not wanting to disturb Molly. As much as he wanted to make love to her again, he wanted more to let her rest, besides—the cat would be watching. There was no telling what the morning would bring—or when they'd have a chance to sleep in a comfortable bed.

Thomas felt as if his eyes had closed for only a second when he was awakened by pounding on the hotel room door.

"Mr. Smith! Wake up!"

Thomas grabbed his jeans and slid into them as he walked to the door. He recognized Miss Lily's voice, and the tone of it didn't bode well. He opened the door a crack.

She narrowed her eyes as she examined him. "I saw your picture on the news. You're an escaped convict."

"I haven't been convicted of anything." Thomas heard Molly stirring behind him. His one thought was to protect her.

"I saw on the news they're after you. They think you killed that woman in Jefferson and her husband down here."

"I didn't kill anyone. What are you going to do?"

"I'm doing it!" She looked past him in the room. "I couldn't help wondering what a killer would be doing with a woman and a cat."

Molly joined him at the door, having donned a robe she must have found in the room. "Miss Lily, we haven't done anything wrong. It was my sister, Anna, who was murdered. Thomas was falsely accused. He didn't do it, and we're trying to find out who did. They took my niece." Molly's voice cracked.

Thomas put his arm around Molly and pulled her against him. "What do you intend to do?" Thomas asked Miss Lily.

"I intend to help you get out of here before the law comes! One of the guests saw you in the dining room last night and he recognized you on the morning newscast. He said he was going to report it to the police and collect the reward they're offering."

"Did he call the police?" Molly asked.

Miss Lily shook her head. "I delayed him as best I could, but you'd best get out of here if you want to stay free."

Molly took the older woman's hand. "Why did you do this?"

"I'm a good judge of character, Mrs. Smith. Your husband isn't a killer. I can tell that right off. And that cat of yours is something else. By the way, I went out this morning and switched the license plates on your car." She held up her hand to stop their comments. "I know a thing or two about evading the law." She laughed at their expressions. "I advise you to change vehicles as fast as you can. Now skedaddle before you end up behind bars."

THE DUST CHURNING UP from beneath the wheels of the car took on a pink cast as the sun rose in the east. Thomas drove fast, heading east again, back to Jefferson. Molly held Familiar in her lap and felt as if the future was closing down on her. It was another of fate's cruel jokes. She and Thomas had been thrown together in a situation that was nothing short of calamitous. After years of guarding her heart, she'd found a man whose inner strength was clear to see. Instead of enjoying dinners and dates and having a chance to get to know him, she was running from the law. And she felt the net closing around them both.

"Thomas, where are we going?"

"I need to call my lawyer, but I don't

want to use the cell phone." He kept his gaze on the road.

"What can your lawyer do to help?"

"I'm not sure anyone can help us, but Mr. Alain said he would do whatever he could for me. Did I tell you he volunteered to represent me because he doesn't believe I'm guilty?"

"He was very helpful when I spoke to him. I just hope he has some suggestions, because we're running out of road." The road sign indicated that a junction with a major highway was two miles ahead. Molly had come to dread intersections. She expected to see a roadblock and a line of lawmen with guns looking for her and Thomas.

"Molly, I just want to tell you that last night was very special to me. Whatever else happens, I wouldn't trade my freedom or my safety for last night."

She reached across the seat to touch his arm. "There are so many things I should tell you about me."

He shook his head. "I know everything I need to know. We're all marked by our past. I accept that. Confessions aren't necessary. I see who you are today, and that's all that matters to me."

"I'm not confessing, but I want you to know that I was married once before. To an artist. Roy Whitehorse. He was the most talented painter I've ever known…" She didn't think she could continue. It was still too painful, even after the time that had passed.

"You don't owe me an explanation, Molly. Not about anything in the past."

"I owe it to myself to tell you." She gazed out the window for a moment, thinking of the images not so unlike the landscape they were driving through that Roy had created. "Roy had incredible talent, but he was a tormented man." She stroked Familiar's back. "I think his art came from his suffering, and after four years of marriage, I decided I couldn't stay." She turned away to watch the scenery pass by the window. "I quit, and I've always despised a quitter."

"Four years seems like a fair amount of time to give a marriage a try. I wouldn't exactly say you were a quitter."

Molly swallowed the lump that rose every time she turned her thoughts to the past. "Roy was devastated. About two months after I moved out, he hung himself. In the suicide note, he said he couldn't live without me."

Thomas slowed the car. "Molly, that was his choice. It had nothing to do with you."

"I know that intellectually. But I feel responsible. He relied on me for so much. When I left…it was awful. He wasn't a man who could live alone."

"So you should sacrifice your life for him?" Thomas pulled the car over at a roadside park. About twenty yards from the pavement was a fast-moving river. "Let's take a walk by the water."

"We need to get out of here. Maybe out of Texas. Or even out of the country." Molly glanced around. She was so used to being on the run that she felt the law was right on her heels.

"Molly, we need to talk about this, and I can't think properly and drive." He opened his door and walked around to hers. "Look, Familiar is ready for a break, too."

The cat darted out of the car and ran toward some willows that leaned over the water and disappeared.

"I don't want to talk about this. I felt I owed you an explanation about why I can't get involved with you. Or anyone else. But it isn't something that's helped by talking about it."

Taking her hand, Thomas led her toward the river. The greenish water rippled over some boulders, and in places where it was shallow, it made a soothing noise. Thomas put his hands on her shoulders. His grip was firm but not tight. "Look at me, Molly."

She forced her gaze up to meet his.

"You're already involved with me. It's too late for second thoughts." He leaned down slowly.

He was going to kiss her. She knew it, yet she couldn't turn away. Even though her instinct was to run as fast as she could from the tangled web of emotions that Thomas represented, she couldn't stop herself. She offered her lips to him, yielding yet again to the power he had over her. She wanted to melt in his arms and allow him to love her. Despite her words of denial, she knew she was involved with him. Deeply involved.

When he broke the kiss, Thomas stroked her hair as he gazed down at her. "Molly, we have a chance at something wonderful. Something so special neither of us can let the hurts and disappointments of the past stop us." He kissed her lips. "And certainly not the guilt."

She leaned into him, taking the comfort that his arms offered. "Roy is the reason I could never confront Anna about her marriage to Darwin. I knew Anna's relationship wasn't good. I knew they had troubles, but how could I advise her when my own husband killed himself?"

Thomas's hands moved up and down her back, soothing her as if she were a child. "Molly, when you left your husband, you did the one thing you could to claim a better life for yourself. You didn't have to talk to Anna. You showed her by example what she needed to do."

His words were so kind and wise that she felt tears sting her eyes. "I should have done more."

He pulled her closer to him. "There was nothing more you could do. I swear that. Not for Roy and not for Anna. Each of us has to assume the burden of responsibility for our own happiness. Anna was doing something. I don't exactly know for sure what she was up to, but she didn't plan on staying with Darwin. That's pretty clear."

"Do you have any idea who Anna might have been involved with? Did she ever mention anyone?"

Thomas cleared his throat. "No, but we have to find out. I think that's the answer to Kate's whereabouts. We have to go back to

Anna's house and look again. There must be something there we missed, something that will give us a clue about her secret life."

"Meow!"

Molly looked down to see Familiar at her feet. His eyes were golden green in the early morning light. "Meow," he said again, blinking twice.

## Chapter Twelve

The small gas station was the only evidence of civilization for miles around, and Thomas pulled to the pumps. He took his last twenty from his wallet and handed it to Molly.

"Would you fill the car up while I make a call?"

"Sure."

He saw the shadow that passed across her face and knew she was fighting to contain her worry. They were on the edge of capture. He knew it, too.

He walked to the pay phone and put the last of his change in the slot when the operator told him the charges for the long distance call to Jefferson. He preferred the pay phone because if the police traced the call, there'd be no way to prove that he'd made it.

The secretary at Bradley Alain's office

answered, and in a few seconds he heard Alain's voice boom into the phone.

"Thomas, where in the hell are you? Most of the state's out searching for you, and if they catch you they won't be gentle."

"I know that," Thomas said. "I need some help, Mr. Alain."

"Call me Bradley. What I can offer as advice is that you find the nearest law enforcement office and turn yourself in. They've implicated you and Molly Harper in the Darwin Goodman murder and as far as the state is concerned, you're on your way to serial killer status."

None of this was good news. Thomas felt as if the hole he was in had just deepened. "I didn't kill anyone. Not Anna and not Darwin."

There was silence on the other end before Bradley spoke again. "For some strange reason I believe you. I think you're innocent. The problem is, the Brownsville police got a call from an eyewitness who put you right at the scene of Goodman's murder. Just tell me you weren't in the Brownsville area. Bring me a witness who can alibi you at some other location. That should be easy enough, and we can get at least the Goodman murder charge dropped."

Thomas sighed. "I was at the motel where Darwin was killed, but I didn't kill him."

"Son, you're in a heap of trouble. Serious trouble. Did you touch anything in that room?"

Thomas tried to remember. Nothing except the door handle. He closed his eyes. His goose was cooked. "Nothing except the door handle." It was best to tell the lawyer everything. Unless he did, Alain couldn't prepare a defense for him.

"That's not good news. What in tarnation were you doing in Darwin Goodman's motel room, especially after you threatened him in the courthouse the day of your arraignment?"

"I was trying to get information about who had really killed Anna. I thought it might have been Darwin."

"Did it ever occur to you that the police are supposed to gather information?"

"They aren't doing a very good job of it." Thomas knew he had to keep his temper in check, but why was he the only one who seemed interested in finding the real murderer?

"Did Darwin tell you anything?"

"Nothing useful," Thomas admitted. He was tempted to tell Alain about the tape recording Molly had, but caution warned him not to drag her into it any deeper than she already was. If he was going to jail for Anna's murder, he might as well do the time for Darwin's, too.

"Where are you, son?"

"I'm on my way back to Jefferson. There's really nowhere else for us to go."

"Do you intend to turn yourself in?"

"I can't." Thomas accepted the box he was in. He couldn't give up trying to prove his innocence, but he was running out of options.

"I have a place outside of town. It's a rental property, but no one is there now. I could—" the attorney paused "—leave the door open for you. But if anyone asks, I'll deny that we ever had this conversation."

Thomas was overwhelmed at the lawyer's willingness to put himself on the line for a man he didn't really know. "Why are you doing this?"

"Let's just say that the wheels of justice often grind too slowly even for a lawyer. Now, the house is north of town on an old ranch road, unpaved. That's why I have such a time renting it. Folks today want pavement up to the door." He sighed. "It's the old Caldwell place. Maybe you know it."

Thomas did indeed. "I know exactly where it is. We should be there sometime today."

"Good, then call me at home and let me know you're safe."

"Got it." Thomas checked his watch. "Thank you, Bradley."

"Thanks aren't necessary. Just get somewhere safe and let's solve this puzzle and find Anna's real killer."

"Thank you."

Thomas felt as if a weight had been lifted from his shoulders. He walked to the car where Molly waited behind the wheel. "You try to sleep and I'll drive. Familiar said he would navigate."

Thomas slipped into the passenger seat and leaned over to kiss Molly soundly on the lips. "My lawyer gave us a place to stay. It's way off the beaten path. I think our luck is finally turning."

THE RANCH HOUSE was at the end of a three-mile, rutted road that cut across rolling fields dotted with black Angus cattle. Molly stared out the window and thought about a time, not so long ago, when paved roads and fast automobiles didn't exist for most people. Nor telephones. This ranch would have been very isolated. Even now she hadn't seen the lights that would indicate a neighbor's house for the past ten minutes.

"This is great." She glanced at Thomas.

"We'll have our privacy, that's for sure." Thomas pulled in front of the house and stopped.

The front porch needed paint, but an old swing creaked gently in the breeze. Molly eased the front door open and stepped into a living room with sparse furnishings. It didn't matter. They had a place to sleep where they could get out of the weather.

A television with rabbit ears was in one corner. "At least we can catch the news," she said. She moved on to the kitchen. The place was immaculate. If they'd thought to bring provisions, they'd be set for a few days at least.

When she returned to the living room, she found Thomas still standing in the same place. "What's wrong?"

"I need to talk to Lou Dial, and I'm not sure I can trust him. Someone had to be able to access your cell phone number to make that call about Kate. That someone is either a person with electronic and technical skills or someone in law enforcement."

"Why do you need to talk to Lou?"

"I need his help on something."

"But you don't know if you can trust him."

"That's right. But we're going to find out right now." He slipped his cell phone from his pocket and dialed.

"Lou, it's Thomas." His gaze never left Molly's as he talked. "Buddy, I need some help."

Molly saw his features harden as Lou spoke.

"I know every law officer in the state is looking for me. Listen, I need some help tracking down some information. McGivens provides computer security for three of the major clothing chains in the area. I need to find out if someone bought a green polar fleece jacket with a hood." He listened to Lou's comments.

"That's right. I know it's a long shot, Lou, but it could really help pinpoint some things. Since McGivens has access to the computers, it wouldn't be difficult for you to check."

Thomas nodded. "I'm near the border and I think the best thing for me is to try to slip across. Maybe make a new life down in Mexico." He listened for a moment. "I can't worry about a baby now. If I don't look out for myself, I'm going to end up in prison." He listened again. "Thanks, and I'll give you a call when I get settled down there." He flipped the phone closed.

"Do you think he'll betray you?" Molly asked.

"I can't be sure." Thomas paced the room. "I just can't be sure. He said all the right things."

Molly sank onto the threadbare sofa. "That's the problem. It could be true, and we don't know one way or the other, but the polar fleece was a great clue. Familiar snagged that piece from the man who attacked you. If we could actually trace it…"

The sound of a vehicle bouncing down the ranch road drew both of them to the window. The black dually pickup truck racing toward them looked ominous. "Do you know the vehicle?" Molly asked.

"Never seen it before. Just act casual. It's our only option."

Together they stepped onto the porch and waited for the truck to stop in the yard beside their car. A tall, distinguished man with dark hair and an impeccable suit stepped out of the truck.

"It's my lawyer," Thomas said. "Bradley Alain. I guess he came to check on us."

The lawyer opened the back door of the

truck and lifted out several plastic sacks. He walked toward them. "I figured you might need a few staples." He held the bags out to them.

Thomas took them. "Thank you, Bradley. This is Molly Harper."

"Miss Harper, so sorry to hear about your sister. And your niece. It's a tragedy to lose a loved one, and I know your grief over the baby must be consuming."

"It is," Molly said. Bradley Alain exuded charm. He was a walking Hollywood version of a distinguished lawyer.

"I met Anna a few times. She'd taken up jogging with my wife, Rachel. I think they were beginning to develop a fast friendship. Rachel is the reason I took on Thomas as a client. Rachel was so upset over Anna's murder and the disappearance of the baby that she badgered me into representing Thomas."

Molly couldn't help but warm to the lawyer. "I'd love to talk to your wife, if she wouldn't mind."

"I'm sure Rachel would be glad to talk to you, but I don't want you to get your hopes up. If she knew something, I think she would have mentioned it to me."

"I just want to talk to her about Anna. My sister might have said something, just a casual remark that gives us a direction to look for Kate."

"I thought the sheriff had determined that the baby was dead." Bradley looked shocked.

"The sheriff believes this, but I don't," Molly said. "There was no evidence Kate was killed. No body has been found."

"Surely Sheriff Johnson wouldn't rush to a rash judgment when a child's life could be at stake." Bradley was clearly appalled at the idea. "Let's step inside and talk this through. If there's a chance a baby is alive and in jeopardy, I want to help you."

Molly stepped inside, and Bradley and Thomas followed. Thomas took the supplies to the kitchen. There was the sound of groceries being unpacked, and Thomas stuck his head around the door frame. "There's coffee in here. I'm going to make a pot. Bradley, can you stay long enough to have a cup?"

"I want to hear all about this baby. A cup of coffee would be nice." The lawyer settled onto the sofa.

Molly took a chair beside him. "Can you help us find Kate?"

The lawyer frowned. "I don't know. I have to have a few more details. The best thing for Thomas would be for us to find that baby and ascertain how she got to where she is. Finding Kate Goodman would go a long way toward clearing Thomas's name."

Molly nodded. "Exactly what I thought."

"Start at the beginning and tell me everything. How did you come to search for the baby?"

"We should wait for Thomas," Molly said. "He'll have some facts to add, I'm sure."

"Without a doubt." Bradley settled back on the sofa. "I must say, you bear a certain resemblance to Anna, but you're nothing like her, are you?"

"Did you know her well?"

"As I said, I met her a time or two. She was a lovely young woman. A little lost I'd say, but very beautiful. I can't say how, but I got the impression she wasn't happy in her marriage."

Molly wanted to roll her eyes but didn't. "Darwin Goodman was abusive. Anna was going to leave him."

"Really. How do you know this?"

"Darwin wasn't Kate's father." Molly saw the surprise on Bradley's face. "Anna was having an affair with someone else. When I find that someone, I'll have a line on Anna's killer and the person who abducted Kate."

"And how do you know all this?" he asked.

At the sound of Thomas entering the room, Molly looked up. She took the cup of coffee Thomas offered her and waited until Bradley had been served and Thomas had returned to the room.

"You asked me how I knew all of this?" she prompted. "I discovered a—"

Before she could finish the sentence, Familiar leaped on the back of the sofa and crashed into Bradley. As the cat gave a startled cry, hot coffee flew everywhere, but mostly onto the lawyer's lap. He yelled and jumped to his feet in obvious pain.

"I'm so sorry," Molly said, rushing to the kitchen for paper towels. She brought back a handful and gave them to the lawyer so he could blot his pants. "I'll be glad to have your suit cleaned."

"Where in the hell did that cat come from?" Bradley demanded.

"He's mine," Molly said. She felt horrible. It was apparent by the lawyer's behavior that he'd been burned by the hot coffee and was in pain. "Familiar didn't mean to spill your coffee."

"That damn cat has scalded me." Bradley was trying hard to hang on to his temper.

"I've never cared for cats." He was slowly regaining his composure. "I'm a dog person."

"Familiar is a unique creature," Thomas said. "He's a—"

Familiar jumped into Thomas's lap, sending his cup of coffee flying into the air. Molly watched in horror as hot liquid spilled down Thomas's chest.

"Dang it!" Thomas jumped up, brushing at his chest. "That's hot!" He gave the cat a glare.

"I'll tell you what that cat is—a nuisance." Bradley walked to the door. "Why don't we finish this conversation tomorrow? In my office. Say noon? My secretaries will be at lunch and you can park in the alley behind my building. No one will see you, and certainly the authorities don't expect you to show up in town again. Just to be on the safe side, I put in a few things you might use for a disguise." He nodded. "We'll talk then. I have some ideas how I may be able to help you." He was out the door when he turned back. "And don't bring that cat."

"Thank you." Molly couldn't think of anything else to say. The man had come to their rescue by offering them the use of his ranch house. He'd stopped by with groceries and help with disguises, and he was just about to help them figure out Kate's disappearance when Familiar had scalded him. She turned to the cat.

"For someone who's supposed to be subtle and sly, that was a big mess. So why didn't you want us to talk to Bradley Alain?"

Familiar gave her a long look.

"I think he finds us amateurish," Molly said.

"No doubt." Thomas stroked the cat. "Bradley is my lawyer, but Familiar is right. We should keep as much as possible to ourselves."

"Meow!" Familiar went to the television and patted it. Molly flipped it on and waited until a commercial finished and a newscast came on. To her surprise, she recognized Miss Lily. A news reporter had a microphone thrust up to Miss Lily's face, and she frowned into the camera.

In answer to the reporter's question, she said, "There was a couple staying here. Mr. and Mrs. John Smith. I didn't see a resemblance to the man the authorities are looking for, but it could be. They said they were headed to California. That's what I told that young couple, John and Judy Adams, when they stopped by this morning asking. They were pushy people, not like the Smiths. But I told the truth, just like I'm telling you folks. The Smiths are gone to California. They're probably in New Mexico by now." She pushed the microphone away and walked off.

"The two missing campers!" Molly turned to Thomas. "They're on our trail."

"I figured they had to be part of the setup. They work for the mastermind behind all of this. It's a good thing we left the Boone Docks when we did."

"Miss Lily is no one to pressure," Molly said with admiration.

"Amen to that." Thomas took her arm. "Let's take a ride up to that state park. Now that I know for certain that the two campers were part of the frame, I want to look for evidence."

"I'm sure the sheriff's men went over the campsite with a fine-tooth comb. If there was something there, they would have found it."

"I agree. But I think we can safely assume that Johnson wasn't looking for anything that might clear me." He took her arm in a gentle grip. "What I'm hoping is that he didn't destroy anything that might help me out."

THEY MADE THE CAMPSITE with enough light for a serious search. Thomas walked slowly among the remains of his camp. A little over a week had passed since he'd been up here, shooting the bull with a couple named John and Judy. He hadn't had a care of the world then, had been completely content to spend the weekend alone beneath the stars. So much had changed in such a short time.

He glanced over at Molly. She was going through the ice chest, one hand covering her nose at the stench of decaying food. Familiar was walking the perimeter of the camp, searching the edge of the woods.

Thomas went to the campfire site and kicked the cold ashes with his boot. It didn't appear that anyone else had used the site— his tent was still there, along with the lantern and other things he'd been forced to leave behind when he was arrested.

Thomas settled onto a log. Most of his life he'd been careful not to put himself in a place where he had to trust another. He thought back to the couple, their easy camaraderie, the subtle way they drew him into conversation. They'd been masters at it—a bit of talk, a card game, conversation about the way Texas was changing—all things he enjoyed.

Someone had done his research on Thomas. He had no doubts now that he'd been deliberately chosen as the scapegoat.

He felt Molly's hand touch his shoulder. "We're going to get to the bottom of all of this," she told him. She sat down beside him and put her hand on his thigh. "Don't give up hope."

"I let down my guard for just a moment with John and Judy. I'm sure there was something in the coffee she gave me. If I could find that coffeepot, I could prove it."

Molly tucked her arm through his. "No, you couldn't."

He gave her a look. "Of course I could. I—"

"If we found the Thermos right this minute, we could never prove *when* the drugs were added. The sheriff would just say that we came up here, found the Thermos and added whatever they find in it. Like we can't prove when we tape-recorded Darwin's murder or the circumstances of it. Finding the coffeepot isn't important. What's important here, Thomas, is that you learn to trust yourself."

Thomas turned to her. Her steady gaze held out a promise to him. "You see some things so clearly. I have implicit trust in myself in business or in work situations. It's only with people that I have a problem."

"You have to trust your judgment, Thomas. Those two campers deceived you. It wasn't your judgment at fault but their motives."

"I trust *you*," he said.

Her smile was slow, but it reached her eyes. "We trust each other."

The black cat rubbed against her shins.

"And Familiar," she added. "We trust him."

"I need to find out if I can trust Lou." Thomas picked up a stick and tapped it against the bottom of his boot.

"So let's go pay a visit to Lou Dial and see what he found out about green polar fleece. Tomorrow I want to talk to Rachel Alain. She may know something about Anna's secret lover."

# *Chapter Thirteen*

Lou Dial held a glass of red wine in his hand as he opened the door. Thomas knew instantly by his stance that Lou had been drinking awhile. Behind Lou the television blared a basketball game. Surprise touched his face and he looked behind Molly and Thomas, as if he expected someone was hiding in the holly bushes beside the house.

Out of the corner of his eye, Thomas saw Familiar slip around the side of the house. While he and Molly questioned Lou, the cat would investigate Lou's home for any clues. Thomas had come to rely on the cat a lot. Familiar would alert them if anything was amiss in the Dial home.

"Hey, man, come in." Lou opened the door wide. "Half the cops in the country are looking for you."

"I know," Thomas said as he stepped into the room.

"I thought you were on your way to Mexico?" Lou glanced at Molly, his gaze curious. "Is this Anna's sister?"

Thomas made the introductions quickly. "Have you talked to Sheriff Johnson lately?"

Lou waved them into chairs as he turned the volume of the television down. "Not lately. Not since you guys split town when he took me up to the courthouse and asked if I knew where you were going. I told him no, and that was the end of it."

"Where does Johnson think I am?" Thomas asked.

"My guess is that he thinks you're headed to the border."

"Why would he think that?" Molly asked.

"Maybe because Darwin Goodman was bumped off in Brownsville, which is a border town, and because you two were implicated in the murder?" Lou gave her a sarcastic look. "So what are you doing back here in Jefferson? It would have been smarter to cross the border and hope the Federales are too busy to chase down an unconvicted American."

Thomas ignored him. "I've been played,

Lou. Someone set me up for Anna's murder and it was someone who knew a lot about me." Thomas realized he sounded hostile and he didn't care.

Awareness touched Lou's face. "You think I set you up?" His voice showed his surprise. "Why would I do that?"

"Good question. I wish I had an answer."

Lou sat down in a big overstuffed chair. He looked at Thomas and then Molly. "You two are getting way too paranoid."

"I've been framed for one murder and implicated in another." Thomas could feel his jaw tightening. "I'm not paranoid, I'm just trying to clear my name of two crimes I had nothing to do with."

Molly stepped forward. "My niece is missing. I know she's alive and I can't find her." She squatted down to Lou's level. "You worked with my sister at McGivens. What can you tell us about her that might make me understand why someone would want to kill her?"

Lou sipped his wine. "Nothing. If there was something to tell, I'd be glad to share." He stared at Thomas. "I'll tell you straight up, man, that I don't appreciate your coming in here and acting like I'm involved in what happened to Anna." He looked at Molly. "Or you either. I liked Anna." He put the glass of wine on the coffee table. "All I tried to do was help you out of a jam. This is pretty pitiful thanks."

Thomas couldn't be certain, but he felt Lou was telling the truth. Lou showed no anxiety or guilt. He was justifiably annoyed. "I'm sorry if I offended you. It's just that this goes from bad to worse. No one is trying to find the truth. I could spend the rest of my life in jail, and an innocent baby has lost her family, if not worse."

Lou rose. "Let me get you both a glass of wine. We can talk this over. There was something Anna said to me at lunch the day before she was killed." He walked into the kitchen and returned with two glasses of wine.

Molly rose to her feet. "What did she say?"

Lou handed her a glass. "She'd gotten into this whole health kick. You know, jogging and going to the gym. She was going to tanning beds, all of that. Made little comments about Antigua and the Cayman Islands, like she was getting ready for a trip. Man, she changed."

"I worked with Anna every day, and she never mentioned going to the islands to me."

Thomas was watching Lou closely. He didn't trust him, but he had no real reason not to. The truth was that he trusted no one except Molly. And Familiar.

"I've known Anna for two years and it seems to me she was always sort of...depressed." Lou glanced at Molly. "Like she was unhappy."

"Did she ever say about what?"

Lou shrugged. "She never said exactly, just a few offhand comments about her husband. And there were the bruises. That was sort of a giveaway." He turned to Thomas. "Don't tell me you never noticed."

"I noticed. Darwin hit her."

Lou shook his head. "She never gave me the details. I think because we were just work friends, she tried harder to keep up a facade. You know, talking about weekend plans, her fitness routine, that kind of thing. Anna was a sweet gal."

"Tell me anything you remember." Molly twirled the wineglass in her hand, but Thomas noticed she hadn't taken a single sip.

"That Friday at work, she was excited about something. She was cleaning out the personal things from her desk. I asked her if she was quitting, and she laughed. She wouldn't say yes or no, but she was so excited. I got the distinct impression she didn't intend to come back to her job."

"Did she have any female friends?" Molly put her wine on the coffee table.

"Not for a long time, but just recently she mentioned a woman named Rachel. One of the joggers."

"Can you remember why she mentioned this Rachel?" Thomas asked.

"Something to do with her training. Like Rachel was helping her get in shape. Nothing sinister, man. I mean, she liked this Rachel chick."

"You never met Rachel?" Thomas asked.

Lou shook his head. "I got the idea from something Anna said that Rachel didn't have a job, that she had lots of free time to work out and lots of money. That's about the extent of it."

Thomas looked past Lou to see Familiar sitting in the front window. The cat nodded once.

"I'm sorry if I offended you, Lou." Thomas put his wine on the coffee table.

"You're in a bad place. I get that. But seriously, man, I only tried to help."

"Did you have any luck on the polar fleece angle?" Thomas didn't hold out much hope, but it didn't hurt to ask.

"Kenneman's carried a top-of-the-line polar fleece jacket that came in a hunter green. It went on sale here back before Christmas. They sold sixty-five extra large jackets." Lou shrugged. "I got a list of the credit card charges." He grinned. "Computer technology is amazing, isn't it?"

Thomas felt a twinge of remorse on how hard he'd been on Lou. The guy had come through with a really difficult task. "Could I look at the list?"

"Sure." Lou got up and brought over a two-page printout. "You know how this kind of list runs. This is only the tip of the iceberg, Thomas. Kenneman's alone probably sold a million of those jackets nationwide. This list is meaningless."

Thomas scanned down it, his gaze stopping on one name. He looked up at Molly. "Anna bought a green polar fleece jacket."

"For Darwin?" Molly asked, stunned.

"Or for someone else. A Christmas present," Thomas said. The impact of his words was hard to miss. "Thanks, Lou. That helped more than you can know."

"I don't see how, but I'm glad I could do something. I wish I could do more, Thomas."

Thomas walked to the door to wait for Molly. "I won't ask you to lie to the authorities, Lou, but if you could avoid talking to the sheriff, I'd appreciate it."

"You got it." Lou held out his hand. "If I can do anything else, call me."

Thomas shook hands. "I hope you understand the position we're in."

Lou turned to Molly. "I liked Anna. I'm sorry this happened, and I hope you find her kid." He walked them to the door and was about to shut it behind them when he stopped. "Oh, yeah. I almost forgot. It might not mean anything, but the day Anna was killed, she had an appointment with someone at the courthouse."

"Did she say who?"

"Nope. She was closemouthed about her business. I sort of figured it might be a lawyer or something. Like she was going to dump her husband."

Thomas saw the look on Molly's face. "Thanks." He took her arm and walked with her to the car. Familiar fell into step behind them.

After he seated Molly, Thomas got in the

car. He could tell the cat had come up empty-handed, but the last tidbit Lou had given them was cause for concern.

"Who do you think Anna was meeting?" Molly asked as he pulled away from the curb.

"We can't know for certain. Lawyers don't really have offices in the courthouse. Just the court officials and the sheriff."

"Sheriff Paul Johnson." Molly's face was grim. "The man who never even searched for Kate. Thomas, every clue we have points to the fact that Johnson is in this up to his eyeballs."

"You don't think Anna was seeing him, do you?" Thomas knew the lawman and Darwin. The two couldn't be more different.

"I can't imagine Anna involved with a law officer. She was always a little on the wild side, but then, who knows? I obviously didn't really know her at all."

Thomas guided the car away from town. Once they left the lights of the city behind them, the sky was a huge black expanse glittering with stars. A crescent moon lay on its back like a smile in the night sky.

"Aren't we going to see Rachel Alain?" Molly asked when she realized they were headed out of town.

"I'm exhausted, and I know you must be,

too." Thomas reached across the car seat and took her hand. "We'll be fresh tomorrow."

"But Kate is out there somewhere."

"I think it would be best if you talked to Mrs. Alain while her husband is at work."

"Why?"

He could feel Molly's gaze on him. "Anna might have been seeing someone, a married man perhaps. And if she confided this to Rachel, she may be reluctant to discuss it in front of her husband."

"Tarred with the same brush?"

"Something like that. I just feel you'd get better information if you spoke with her alone."

"Good thinking." Molly settled back into the seat.

Two minutes later, when Thomas looked at her, she was sound asleep, her head back against the car seat. Familiar snuggled at her side, purring as he, too, slept.

No matter what it took, Thomas knew that he would protect this woman and the cat. Whatever else happened, he would keep them safe.

MOLLY AWOKE when she felt herself lifted in strong arms. She reached up with her palm and touched Thomas's face as he carried her.

A sense of safety and contentment settled over her. She knew where she was, and she knew how high the stakes were, but Thomas was there. And Familiar.

When Thomas eased her into the bed, she reached out and caught his hand. "Don't leave me," she said, still half-asleep. "Tell me you won't leave me."

"I'm right here." He sat on the bed beside her.

The house was cold and she shivered. That was all it took for Thomas to slip beside her in the bed. "Do you need more blankets?"

"No." She looked at him in the starlight. His hazel eyes stared into hers as if he could never see enough of her. "There are other methods of getting warm." His smile was worth a million dollars.

"I thought you were exhausted."

"I'm tired of running and being afraid, but I'm not too tired to make love." She sat up and kissed him, a fiery, passionate kiss that left no doubt as to her intentions. His response was instantaneous. In a moment he was removing her clothes, and then his.

"Thomas, if we hadn't been forced into each other's company, do you think we would have dated each other?"

"Dated?" He laughed. "What's that?"

She touched his lips and felt the smile there. "It's a word from another reality, isn't it? I used to date. I used to go out to dinners and plays. I feel like I was another person then."

"When I was on the range, I used to think about a woman I'd want to date. Out there in the dark, I could dream up the perfect woman."

"What was she like?"

His lips found hers, and the kiss was sweet and tender. "She was almost as perfect as you." He kissed her again, this time with more heat. "Almost, but not quite."

When he kissed her the third time, Molly forgot about cowboys and fantasies. The moment with Thomas was far too intense to think of anything else.

*I'M GLAD THE TWO HUMANOIDS have found some comfort in each other's arms. This has been a long, hard few days. And those two, with their blabbermouths yakking to that lawyer, aren't making it any easier for me.*

*I realize that Bradley Alain is Thomas's lawyer and the man Thomas has chosen to trust. But that's not true for Molly and me. The man's slick. That can be a plus for a lawyer, but it sure makes a cat's hair stand on end. I'd rather take the wait-and-see approach, especially since I know as an officer of the court he really can't risk helping us much more than he already has. He could lose his license for what he's done. I just see it as too much risk for too little potential return.*

*On a more positive front, when we find Kate and the real killers, I'm going to send Miss Lily a bouquet of roses. Or maybe lilies! I don't think she actually threw anyone off our scent, but she surely didn't give us away and managed to warn us that the missing campers are hot on our heels. What a lady. Maybe when I retire I can move down and be the official cat at the Boone Docks.*

*I scoped out Lou Dial's home and found nothing to lead me to believe he's involved in this. His vehicle was clean, his trash normal stuff. I looked in every window and saw only the regular bachelor mess. When I listened to his conversation with Thomas and Molly, I had the sense he was telling the truth. Of course humanoids can be pretty tricky. I haven't ruled him completely off my suspect list, but he's way at the bottom.*

*I hope tomorrow yields some fruit in this case. It's pointless to tell Molly that every day that passes lessens the chance that we'll find Kate. What puzzles me is the person who wrote and called, revealing that the baby is still alive. What does this person hope to gain? Obviously, she knows that Kate is related to Molly. And she's trying to return the baby to her relative. But why? What's in it for her?*

*What's in this for Sheriff Johnson? Now that's a man I'd like to have a conversation with. A long, intimate one. If he had something to tell, I'd get it out of him and sharpen my claws at the same time. I just have the sense that he knows more about Anna's murder and Kate's disappearance than he's telling anyone.*

*He never really looked for Kate. And no one has stepped up and pointed this out. Everyone acts like Kate is dead. Why?*

*I'll ponder that question tonight in my subconscious. Right now I'm going to see if that lawyer brought any vittles fit for a cat. Then I'm going to curl up on the sofa and sleep. Tomorrow is another day, and maybe we'll catch a break in this case.*

*Sweet dreams, humanoids. Rest easy in the comfort of love while I dream of my sweet and patient Clo-tilde back in Washington, D.C., waiting for me. I have to admit that I'm getting a little too old for this life. I miss my lady-love and the home-cooked meals my humanoids prepare for me. I'll just have to solve this case and get home.*

BRIGHT SUNLIGHT through the curtainless window awakened Molly. She felt marvelous in a way she'd never felt in her life before. She sat up, unable to resist touching Thomas's lean back. The sight of him made her want to make love again, but instead she slipped from the bed and padded barefoot to the bathroom. The house was freezing. During the night the temperature had dropped, and though the sun was bright, the air was not warm.

Familiar was asleep on the sofa, and she stroked the top of his head. He gave her a yawn and a purr. "Meow?"

She stopped and looked at him. She could almost swear that he had said "breakfast." Bradley had brought eggs and bacon, and she rustled up a quick meal for the cat. Familiar dove into the bacon with pleasure, but she could see he had lost a bit of weight. When she went into town to talk to Rachel, she'd stop by a fish market and get something fresh and wonderful for the cat. She bent to stroke his back and was rewarded with a kiss on her shin.

While Thomas was sleeping, Molly called her answering service at home to check for any new messages. The last call about Kate had come through on her cell phone, and Molly held little hope that there was another communication, but it didn't hurt to check.

She put in the code to key the answering service to replay messages, taking two about work and one from a friend who was concerned about her. There was nothing from the stranger who had sent information about Kate.

Molly reached into her pocket and found the note that had been sent to her about Kate—the note that had incited her search. It was just a thin piece of paper, but it was the first tangible proof she had that her niece might be alive. With each incident that happened, she was more and more positive that Kate was alive. Finding her was the issue. No matter how long it took, though, she would find Kate and raise her and love her. No one would ever replace Anna, but Molly would give it a hundred percent.

She hung up her phone and went to the television in the front room. Familiar followed her and jumped on the sofa as she turned on the local news. She was shocked to find her photograph on the screen.

"A Phoenix, Arizona, woman is wanted in the murder of Darwin Goodman. Jefferson County Sheriff Paul Johnson has issued a statement saying that Molly Harper has been connected to both the murder of Goodman and the jailbreak of Thomas Lakeman, who is wanted in the murder of Harper's sister, Anna Goodman."

The reporter kept talking while Molly watched in horror as footage of her Phoenix, Arizona, home came on the screen with police officers breaking down the door.

"I guess they found your fingerprints in Darwin's motel room," Thomas said.

He was standing in the doorway. He'd slipped into his jeans and a flannel shirt, warding off the chill of the house.

"I can't believe this is happening." She sounded as if she was lost. "How could anyone believe I'd do such a thing?"

He came to her and held her. "I'm so sorry, Molly."

"Me, too. You know I didn't kill Darwin, but I was there. I wish people would listen to us. The real killers are running free."

He stroked her back and she felt herself begin to relax. "Molly, it's going to be okay. Let's go and see Rachel Alain. Maybe she can shed some light on this for us."

## *Chapter Fourteen*

Rachel Alain was almost the exact opposite of what Molly had expected. In her mind she'd visualized a tall, rangy redhead who had the lean muscles of a marathon runner. Instead, Rachel was a petite blonde with apple cheeks and a curvaceous figure. She opened the door to Molly's knock with a frown on her face. "What do you want?"

Despite her lack of graciousness, Molly smiled. "I think you knew my sister."

Rachel's expression didn't change. "There's nothing I can tell you. My husband is risking a lot to try and help Thomas. There's nothing else I can do." She started to close the door.

"Wait!" Molly put out her hand and stopped the door. "I just want to talk about Anna."

Clearly uncomfortable, Rachel stepped back and allowed her to enter. "I'll talk to you, but only for a minute. I was getting ready to join some friends for a run." Her outfit confirmed the statement. She was dressed in running shorts and shoes and a tank top. "Follow me into the den."

"I won't detain you, I promise." Molly followed her down a long dark hallway and into a comfortable room with two leather sofas. She sat opposite Rachel. "It's just that I'm having trouble finding any of Anna's friends. Your name kept coming up as someone who was helping Anna get into shape, and I thought I'd ask if she said anything to you that might help me find the baby."

"Sheriff Johnson says Katie is dead." Rachel's voice was flat as she spoke, and she looked down at the floor.

Although the words were like knives in Molly's heart, she smiled. "I don't believe that. I think Kate is still alive, and I'm going to find her."

"I hope what you believe is true, but my husband tells me otherwise. He says there's proof Kate is…gone."

"From what I've seen, there isn't really proof. In my opinion the sheriff and his deputies jumped to the conclusion that Kate was dead. That was the convenient decision. The decision that required no work or effort in putting on a search."

"There was a search, Miss Harper. I don't know how to tell you this." Her gaze was steady and her voice without real inflection. "Sheriff Johnson issued a statement that footsteps led from Thomas Lakewood's house to the Cypress River. His conclusion was that Kate was thrown into the river and her body was eventually swept out to the Gulf. He said it would be impossible to recover the body and that he wasn't going to spend endless hours of manpower on what would be a futile effort. He's the law in Jefferson County, and he believes Katie is dead. I can't help you. I liked Anna, and I'm sorry for what happened. You have to leave, though." She wiped a fine mist of perspiration from her forehead though the room was cool.

Molly felt her heart thud. "Please, I need your help." On the end table was a photograph of Anna holding Kate. Rachel stood beside Anna, a big smile on her face as she held one of Kate's booties.

Rachel took a deep breath. "You may view Sheriff Johnson as a hick sheriff, part of a small-town law enforcement organization, but he's a good lawman." She no longer attempted to look up from her lap.

"I'm not trying to disparage the sheriff." Molly dragged her gaze from the photograph and forced a smile. "Rachel, I just want to find my niece. I lost my sister, and I don't want to lose Kate." She had no doubt Rachel knew something, but she didn't want to press the woman into a corner or she might never help.

Rachel twined her fingers together and then dropped her hands in her lap. "What do you want to talk about?"

"I've heard from a couple of people that Anna wasn't happy in her marriage. Did she ever mention any of that to you?"

Rachel's look was quick, surprised. She tried to cover it, but she was too late. "She wouldn't confide that sort of thing to me. Anna never discussed her personal life. Not with anyone."

Molly didn't believe her. "You're the closest thing to a girlfriend Anna had. Surely she talked to you."

"You're her sister. Didn't she talk to you?" Rachel snapped.

It was another direct hit on her heart, but Molly only nodded. "I feel that I abandoned Anna. You don't need to point that out."

"I'm sorry. I didn't mean that. It's just that..." She looked around the room, then at the photograph on the end table. She closed her eyes. "There's no point lying. Anna told me she was leaving Darwin. She never really talked about her marriage, but she did confide in me that she was leaving. I was very fond of Anna and Katie. And I worried about both of them. Anna often had bruises. She said before Kate came, Darwin was even more brutal toward her. The baby softened him."

"Was Kate Darwin's child?"

Rachel looked puzzled. "Of course. Anna never mentioned anything to the contrary."

"No hints?" Molly waited.

A frown touched Rachel's face. "Now that you mention it. Maybe she did. I just didn't pick up on it."

"What did she say?"

"That sometimes a man or woman couldn't honor their word." She paused. "That circumstances sometimes made people do things that were dishonorable and cruel to others." Rachel looked up. "I think she was trying to tell me she was having an affair. She was testing to see how I'd react."

"I think you're right. Do you have any idea who she might have been seeing?"

Rachel shook her head. "Not any of the joggers. I would have noticed that, even if I had been obtuse about her affair."

"Then who?"

"Someone at work?" Rachel asked.

"Maybe, but I don't think so. What about the sheriff?"

"Paul?" Rachel almost laughed. "I couldn't imagine it. He's a good-looking guy, but he lives and breathes that job. I don't believe he has time for his wife, much less an affair. If he was involved with Anna, he wouldn't have been so quick to pull back the search for Kate."

"Unless he killed Anna and took the baby." Molly was risking a lot by putting her theory out there, but she had to see Rachel's reaction.

Rachel's eyes filled with tears. "I can't discuss this." She walked to the door. "You have to leave, Miss Harper."

"Do you believe Paul Johnson is capable of killing my sister and taking their child?"

"I don't believe Paul is Kate's father."

Rachel was walking a thin line, not wanting to deny Johnson's involvement, but limiting it. "Any suggestions who Kate's father might be?"

Rachel retrieved the photograph. For a long moment she looked at it. "The only person I see in Katie is her mother. Other than that, I can't tell you anything. Please leave. You've only upset me and there's nothing I can do to help you."

Molly felt as if her last hope had been exhausted. She rose slowly. "Thank you for talking with me. I'll let you get on with your day." She turned to leave the room. "Ms. Alain, who took that photograph?"

"My husband." She hesitated. "Don't give up your search for Kate."

Molly faced her. "Is there something else you know?"

Rachel looked stricken. "Oh, no. It's just that I'd know if Katie were dead—I'd feel it. But she's alive. Even if you never find her, know that she's alive."

"Mrs. Alain, she's my niece. I want to love her and raise her and tell her all the stories I know about her mother. Kate is my flesh and blood, and I want her back."

Rachel walked to her and touched her hands. "I couldn't agree more." She walked past Molly and held the front door open. "If I think of something I'll give you a call. Leave me a number where you can be reached."

Molly wrote down her cell phone number and left. Familiar and Thomas were waiting for her at the ranch. She'd left them there with no means of transportation. Now it was time to pick him up and make the appointment with Thomas's lawyer and Rachel's husband. Molly had the feeling that Bradley knew more than he'd let on.

As PROMISED, Bradley had cleared his office of all personnel. When Thomas and Molly walked in, he personally escorted them to his private quarters—a large, bookshelf-lined office with a view of downtown. Two chairs had been placed in front of his desk. He indicated they were to sit there.

"Did you talk with Rachel?" Bradley asked.

"I did."

"Was she helpful?"

"A little." Molly had recovered a bit from her disappointment. "She didn't know a lot. She's going to try to remember conversations, things like that."

"Rachel is a very kind woman. It's one of her best traits." He leaned back in his chair. "I've been giving your predicament some thought, Thomas. I urge you again to turn yourself in."

Thomas shook his head. "I didn't kill Anna. Nor did I have anything to do with Darwin Goodman's death."

Bradley templed his fingers. "I guess you know the police found Molly's fingerprints at the motel where Darwin was killed." He looked at Molly. "I'm just curious. Why were your fingerprints on file?"

"When I took the job at the reservation, they had to run a background check. They checked my fingerprints to be sure I didn't have a criminal record under another name."

He nodded. "Tough break." He turned to Thomas. "I talked with Paul Johnson this morning. He's moving the hunt for the two of you to the next level. You've angered him, Thomas. You've made him look like a fool, and that's a hard thing for an elected official to live down."

"My jailbreak wasn't aimed at making Johnson look stupid. I'm trying to find Anna's killers."

"I know that and you know that, but it seems no one else knows that or even wants to entertain the possibility."

"You said you had some ideas about what we should do?" Molly sat up straight in her seat. "What were you thinking?"

"I had a conversation with the sheriff about that baby. He said all of the evidence wasn't released to the public, but that he had no doubt the infant was dead. Kate was drowned. You have to accept that." He looked directly into Molly's eyes as he talked. "Ms. Harper, I know this isn't what you want to hear, but I think you should listen. Chasing after your niece has put you in line for a murder conviction. You and Thomas need to stop this. All you've succeeded in doing is stepping into the middle of Darwin's murder and you're not a step closer to finding Kate Goodman because she isn't alive."

Molly felt as if he were striking her with a heavy hammer. Each word broke a little bit more off her hope that Kate was alive and that she could find her and save her.

"We will find Kate." Thomas rose to his feet quickly. "And we will find the people who killed Anna and Darwin. I'm going to clear my name. I don't care if I have to spend the rest of my life hunting, I'll find that baby and clear my name."

Molly felt such a rush of love for Thomas that she couldn't speak. She swallowed the lump of emotion in her throat and looked at him. "Thank you," she said. She stood beside him. "If you don't have any other suggestions, we should get out of town."

"You can't continue to run. Eventually the law is going to catch you, and I'm afraid it's going to be a bloodbath. Let me call Paul and get him over here. He can be a reasonable man. Bond will be set and I'll help you both make it."

Thomas put his arm around Molly. "We'll continue until we find the truth, or until someone stops us."

The telephone on Bradley's desk began to ring. "Hold up just a second," he said as he reached for the phone. "Bradley Alain here."

Molly saw his face blanch. He didn't utter a sound but simply returned the telephone to its cradle. His hand shook. He turned to her. "Rachel's been murdered. Someone attacked her while she was jogging." His features hardened. "You were the last one to talk to her. You were the last one to see her alive."

THOMAS GRASPED MOLLY'S ARM and forced her out of the law office. She was in shock. She seemed to be in some sort of trance, unable to think or move. He finally scooped her into his arms and carried her out of the building and to the car. When he opened the door, she got in slowly, as if she'd never done such a thing before.

"We'll figure this out, Molly." He spoke soothingly to her as he backed out of the alley and onto the street. When they'd come to Bradley's office, Molly had driven and he'd hidden in the back seat. Now he was behind the wheel. If anyone recognized him, it could present serious problems.

He looked around for Familiar. The cat had refused to go to the lawyer's office. Instead, he'd taken off down the street toward the courthouse and the sheriff's office. Now Thomas wished him to magically appear. They needed to find a safe place and regroup. If Bradley really thought Molly had killed his wife, it would be only a matter of time before the lawyer called the sheriff and told him where he and Molly were staying. Judging by the look on Bradley's face when he'd turned to Molly, he did think Molly had hurt Rachel.

They had to get the cat and get out of town.

He pulled a baseball cap Bradley had brought them down low over his face, turned the corner and headed west, away from the courthouse. If Familiar wasn't around, they'd have to leave him. It was a tough decision—

Thomas had grown to respect the cat and his abilities—but they couldn't risk capture.

"Molly?" Thomas touched her hand gently. "Molly?" She looked as if she'd lost all vitality. He had to snap her out of it. "Molly, talk to me. We have to think this through and get out of town."

"I know."

He glanced at her with relief. She was coherent. "I had to leave Familiar in town. Maybe we can swing back by and try to find him. But we get our things and get out of here."

"I know."

He slowed the car. Molly sounded like she was a zombie. "Molly, honey, snap out of it. I need your help."

"I didn't kill Rachel. I didn't. I swear it. But wherever I go, people die. Maybe it's best that I don't find Kate."

He looked around at the rolling fields dotted with black Angus cattle. This was a land he knew and loved. His biggest dream had been to earn enough money to buy his own spread, a place where he could raise some horses, marry a good woman and have a couple of children. It wasn't a dream of great wealth or luxury. It was more about hard work and a goal that included a way of life. Now he could see that was forever out of his reach. By some wretched quirk of fate, he'd been cast as a murderer. Everything he'd worked for was gone, and now his freedom would be lost if he was captured.

He looked at Molly and knew that, despite all that he most probably stood to lose, loving her was worth all the risk. He loved her. Even as she sat beside him in the car crying silently. He loved her strengths and her weaknesses, and it was killing him that he couldn't protect her from the events that had railroaded their lives.

He stopped the car. "Molly, we can't leave Familiar in town. We have to go back and get him."

Molly wiped the tears from her face. "Let's go."

"We may be arrested." He picked up her hand and squeezed it. "We're not cut out to be Bonnie and Clyde. This life of being on the run is wearing me down, but I don't see another option."

She took a deep breath and sat up. "There is no other choice. We have to evade capture if we can. I certainly don't feel like Bonnie, but I'm going down fighting."

When she turned to look at him, tears still

hanging in her thick lashes, he saw that she meant every word. She was resilient and determined, and he loved her even more.

*I SAW THOMAS AND MOLLY beating a hasty retreat from that lawyer's office. I wonder what the heck happened. Thomas was driving like a bat out of hell, and Molly looked like she'd been hit in the head with an ax. Stunned, in other words. I was on the second floor of the courthouse trying to get into the sheriff's private office. By the time I could have gotten outside to try and flag down my ride, Thomas and Anna would have been almost to the ranch.*

*So I opted to stay here and explore. And wouldn't you know it, the entire sheriff's office exploded like a cherry bomb in an ant bed. Deputies flew out the door with Sheriff Paul Johnson leading the herd. And he left his door wide-open for me to enter.*

*I'm a curious cat—something that's caused me no end of problems in the past, but I haven't been able to break myself of the habit of snooping.*

*Here's Johnson's desk. I wish I could hear the call that sent them all running out of here, but I'll worry about that later. Right now I need to search for reports. Hmm, the autopsy on Anna is right here on top. Gunshot wound to the heart, no big surprise there.*

*There was bruising on her neck, too. Now that's new information. Goes along with the stories about Darwin's brutality, but what it doesn't jibe with is Thomas's observations that she was excited and happy the last time he saw her. There must be autopsy photographs, and though I'm not fond of looking at such tragic pictures, it must be done. Here they are. And I clearly see the fingerprints on her neck. I wonder if anyone attempted to get prints. There should be a report and here it is.*

*These things aren't hard to read. Let's see, the marks on her neck were printed with some success. Oh, my. This would have helped a lot, if someone had bothered to tell us. The prints on her neck don't belong to Darwin. Someone else was trying to choke Anna!*

## Chapter Fifteen

Thomas parked the car behind the library. Molly, hair in braids and wearing big sunglasses, had gotten out at the other end of town. Their goal was to find the cat and leave as quickly as possible—without getting arrested.

The day was sunny but cold, and Thomas's breath huffed out in front of him as he walked. He pulled the visor of his ball cap down lower and tightened the hood of his sweatshirt so that little of his face was exposed. A four-day growth of beard softened the line of his square jaw.

The streets of Jefferson were quiet, as if all sensible people were inside at work or home. It was a pretty town with friendly people, and Thomas realized that he'd come to view it as home. Today he felt like an outcast. He was someone that children would be afraid of. It was a painful realization.

He kept walking. "Familiar." He called the cat, disdaining the "kitty, kitty" that most people used. Familiar wouldn't answer to such foolishness. He was a private investigator, not some ordinary cat.

Thomas passed a beauty shop, a bar and a grocery, and when he came to a corner florist, he heard the cry of a cat. He stepped inside the opening of a wire-enclosed greenhouse area, finding himself on a porch covered in exotic and beautiful plants.

"Meow."

Though he listened hard, he couldn't tell where the cat was hiding. There were a million hiding places, and the animal sounded weak, frail. Had something happened to Familiar? Was that why he hadn't shown up?

"Familiar?" He knelt to look under some trailing ferns. The cry might have come from there.

"Can I help you?"

Thomas looked up into the face of a young woman who stood with a bunch of daisies in her hand. "I thought I heard a cat." He stood up. "It sounded sick."

"There's a stray kitten hanging around here. I've tried to give it away, but no one wants it. I already have fifteen cats, and I just can't take on another one."

Thomas was about to stand up when a tiny white head with gray ears poked out of the fern. Bright green eyes gazed at him.

"She's not going to last much longer if she doesn't find a warm home," the woman said. "It's supposed to get down to twenty degrees tonight."

Thomas held the kitten, who purred outrageously in his hand.

"I've lost a big black cat. You haven't seen him hanging around here, have you?"

The woman shook her head. "No black cats, just that kitten."

The woman's steady gaze unnerved Thomas and he left the florist shop hurriedly. As he stepped onto the street, two women strolled toward him. He ducked back around the corner, walking away from Main Street. Eventually he would have to confront someone. If that someone recognized him, he most likely wouldn't escape being captured by the law. Molly faced the same risk as she searched for Familiar.

He called Familiar again, trying hard not to think of the tiny kitten. He sighed and kept walking.

"Familiar." He stopped beside an alley.

"Meow."

This was the cry of a full-grown, healthy cat, and Thomas felt his hopes rise. He hadn't realized just how worried he was about the cat. "Come on, boy, we've got to find Molly and get out of town. Rachel Alain was murdered—they're going to try to pin that on Molly."

Familiar appeared from the depths of the alley with a photograph in his mouth. For a moment Thomas was so shocked at the graphic autopsy photograph of Anna that he couldn't move. Where had Familiar gotten the photograph, and why did he have it? Molly couldn't see this. She couldn't. It would destroy her.

He took the picture from the cat's mouth and stuffed it inside his jacket. Later, when they were out of town, he'd figure out what Familiar was doing with it. He started to walk away, but he felt Familiar's paw snag his pants leg.

"We have to make tracks." Thomas pointed down the street where the town's businesses faded into residential. "We'll be safer down there, away from Main Street."

Familiar blinked once and followed at

Thomas's heels as they walked the three blocks and ducked into a copse of trees beside a beautiful river—the river where the sheriff said Kate had drowned. Hidden from view from the street, Thomas took out the photograph and sat on the ground beside Familiar.

"Meow." Familiar batted the photograph, his paw touching the marks on Anna's neck.

"I see that." Thomas felt rage rising up in him. Darwin was such a jerk. He must have hurt Anna, forcing her to run to Thomas's house, where she was killed. "I'm glad Darwin is dead."

Familiar's paw dug into his thigh.

"Yeow!" Thomas almost jumped up. "I get the point that you didn't like what I said, but I'm not sure which part." He thought about it. "I'm glad he's dead?"

Familiar blinked once.

"Darwin?"

Familiar blinked twice and then gave him a head-butt of success.

"You're saying Darwin didn't try to choke Anna?"

Familiar stood on Thomas's thigh and licked his face.

"Then who did?"

The cat stepped back and stared at him with an unblinking gaze.

"You don't have that answer. But if it wasn't Darwin, was it the killer?" Again the cat had no answer. "Or is it more likely the person who did this was her lover?" Thomas saw the many possibilities Familiar's new information gave them. It was their first real lead, if they could only determine who had hurt Anna.

He put the picture back in his jacket. "If you know positively it wasn't Darwin, that means the deputies lifted prints from Anna's neck and tried to match them to Darwin's prints." He looked down at Familiar. "And mine! They wouldn't match my prints, either! Why wasn't I ever told about this? Why wasn't my lawyer told?"

Familiar did a figure-eight around Thomas's legs.

"Let's get Molly," Thomas said. He checked his watch. If he hustled he would be on time to make the rendezvous point.

MOLLY SAW THEM COMING and felt her mood lift. She'd been worried about Thomas and Familiar. They'd run a big risk coming back to town, but now she felt they could possibly escape. Where in the heck had Familiar gone?

Thomas swept her into his arms and gave her a huge kiss. "Familiar has found a terrific lead," he said. "And now I know what I have to do to get the rest of the information we need. Sheriff Johnson has been holding back facts, and I believe I can prove it."

Molly nodded. "What are you going to do?"

Thomas looked down at Familiar. "We're going to break into the sheriff's office."

"What, you're afraid they aren't smart enough to catch you without help?" Surely he was teasing. If he tried to do that, he'd be caught.

"Familiar found a photograph of Anna." He put his arm around Molly and hugged her. "It's an autopsy photo, Molly. You don't want to see it. There are marks on her neck, like someone tried to strangle her. Familiar has discovered that the prints they took from Anna's neck don't belong to Darwin or to me! Yet I was never told about this and neither was my lawyer."

"Sheriff Johnson is covering up for someone."

"And it isn't Darwin."

"So who could it be?"

"It's not looking good for the sheriff. He

had to have been involved. He's been able to choreograph every move of the murders and the investigation."

Molly felt the skin of her neck ripple with goose bumps. She'd suspected the sheriff was involved all along. Now that his role was confirmed, it made her realize how vulnerable she and Thomas were if they were captured. Johnson could rig any evidence to show their guilt. He could take false statements. He could have been the one to take the baby.

"Thomas, our situation is precarious."

"Especially if they charge you with Rachel's murder."

Molly closed her eyes for just a moment. It was almost impossible to believe that the woman she'd visited only that morning was dead. She'd had the sense that Rachel was holding something back from her, and now she'd never know what that might be. "Do you think Bradley will continue to represent you?" she asked.

"I have serious doubts that I can find legal representation for five hundred miles around. The Alains were well thought of." He shrugged. "Did you notice anyone around when you left the Alain house?"

"No." She thought about it. "Rachel was killed jogging. Or that's what Bradley said, remember?"

"That's right. Maybe someone was watching the house, though. If you saw anything…"

Molly focused on the morning just past. "A car did pass on the street when I was leaving, and it seemed maybe Rachel had recognized the person driving it. Even so, what does that prove? It's useless information."

"Someone saw you leaving and she was alive."

"And I could have gone back and killed Rachel ten minutes later." She couldn't hide the dejection she felt.

"I'm going to get the evidence we need. With Familiar's help. Please wait for us behind that old drive-through dry cleaners. I need to get the file on Anna's murder."

"Thomas, that's asking for trouble."

"I'll be back. Just be behind the dry cleaners and ready to run."

"I'll be there." She kissed his lips lightly. "Why would someone want to kill Rachel?"

"Maybe because she knew something they were afraid she'd tell you."

Molly swallowed the anger that rose in her throat. Not at Thomas, but at the person who was so ruthlessly killing those who got in his or her way. People like Rachel Alain. She'd said that Kate was alive. She'd said it as if she knew it.

"Instead of the sheriff's office, do you think we can break into the Alain home?"

"Why?" Thomas's confusion showed clearly on his face.

"I may be wrong, but I think Rachel knows…knew where Katie is. I've been giving it a lot of thought, and I think she may have been the person who sent me that note and called. She was so nervous when I was at her home, as if she were afraid to talk. I think she wanted me to find Katie. She wanted me to keep looking and not give up. Maybe she was involved in something bad, something that Anna got caught up in."

"Why do you say that?"

"It's a gut feeling." Molly shook her head. "I don't think I can justify it with facts."

She saw Thomas considering. "I need to get those records from the sheriff's office. Most of the deputies are likely working Rachel's murder now. I may never have an opportunity like this again."

She nodded. "I'll be waiting for you."

He kissed her, and she finally understood

the concept of longing for another person. She longed for a hour alone with Thomas, for a conversation that wasn't fraught with danger, for a meal where they could laugh and talk about a future with promise instead of possible jail terms—or worse, lethal injections. If she was convicted of Rachel Alain's murder, she would get the needle.

"Are you sure you're okay?"

"I'm fine." She smiled. "Get those records, and by then maybe the Alain house will be a little easier to break into."

WITH FAMILIAR at his side, Thomas hurried toward the courthouse. The sheriff's office was on the ground floor, with the jail attached as a separate wing. The courthouse also contained the clerks for civil and criminal courts and several other public offices. Normally it was a busy place with folks paying taxes or looking up land deeds. There was a back entrance to the sheriff's office, though, one that was used by the deputies. Thomas knew this because he'd had a friend who was a deputy for a brief time.

He found the door and eased it open, surprised that it was unlocked. The deputies had gone on the call to the Alain murder with such speed they'd forgotten to lock the door.

Familiar slipped in beside him and together they walked toward the main office. The cat had been able to get inside without much trouble. It was going to be more difficult for Thomas to escape notice.

When he got to the door that led to the suite of offices, Thomas eased it open and listened. A dispatcher was sitting at a desk reading a book. She seemed completely absorbed in her story. Easing into the room, he followed Familiar into an office marked with Paul Johnson's name and title.

The office was reasonably neat, Thomas noticed. It was a telling thing about Johnson. In his years in Jefferson County, Johnson had been a popular sheriff, one who solved the burglaries and vandalism of a normally quiet county. The crime rate in the area was low. Lately, though, Johnson had been hopping.

Thomas sat down at the sheriff's desk and began to search through the files in his desk drawers. It made sense that the case, which was recent, hadn't been archived yet. He searched through two drawers before he turned his attention to the clutter on top of Johnson's desk. The file was there. Time was crucial, but Thomas had to find evidence. He went through the autopsy pictures, his throat constricting with emotion at what had been done to Anna.

He scanned the scenes carefully. Familiar had done a thorough job. The most telling photograph was the one showing the bruises on Anna's neck. He was tempted to replace the photo that Familiar had taken, but he kept it instead. Johnson could make evidence disappear if he chose to. Thomas couldn't risk it. He also picked up the report that showed the fingerprints on Anna's neck were not Darwin's. The report said the prints had not found a match in the criminal files—and Thomas's prints had been taken when he was first arrested.

An outsider? Thomas considered. Maybe, maybe not. He continued through the stack of papers, reading statements from witnesses, even his own. Time was ticking by. He could almost feel the sheriff drawing closer and closer. He had to hurry. If there was anything to find, he had to find it fast.

He went through the entire case file. There was no mention of John and Judy, the other campers. No attempt had been made to find them—because they were part of the setup.

Darwin's statement was interesting. He accused Thomas of sleeping with Anna and of killing her. But his words didn't ring true, even on the page. Darwin had never suspected Anna of cheating on him. Not really. Or at least that was what he'd told Molly just before he died. He'd said Anna was too afraid of him to cheat on him.

The truth had been twisted and turned so that he, Thomas, looked guilty. He saw clearly how Johnson was distorting some facts, omitting others. Johnson had gathered only the evidence that could be used to build an airtight case against Thomas. There had been no real effort to find Anna's killer or even look for Kate. Thomas wanted nothing better than to find Johnson and beat the living thunder out of him.

Still, the question was *why*. Why had Anna been killed? What had prompted it, if it wasn't Darwin's jealous rage? The answer to that question would be found once they discovered who her lover had been. That was likely what Rachel Alain had known. That's what had gotten her killed. And what would get Molly killed, if Thomas wasn't smart enough to prevent it.

He had to get out of the sheriff's office

and get back to Molly. He had to find a safe place for her, somewhere she could hide out until he figured this out.

He arranged the files the way he'd found them. On the off chance he'd missed something, he opened a few drawers. He heard the door open and his heart stopped.

"Thomas Lakeman, you're under arrest."

Thomas looked up into the cold blue eyes of Sheriff Paul Johnson. The gun Johnson held was trained on Thomas's heart.

"Put the photograph down," Johnson said. "Turn around slowly with your hands behind your back. This time you're going to jail and you're going to stay there."

## *Chapter Sixteen*

From the secluded safety of an oak tree, Molly watched the town businesses and shops close. It was five o'clock. Thomas had been gone over two hours. He was in trouble. More trouble than Familiar could get him out of—otherwise they would both be at her side.

She was afraid to go into the courthouse to look for him. There was no one she could call to help. She had to assume that Thomas had been caught, and now it was up to her. In her heart she knew Kate was alive and that Rachel Alain had known it, too. She knew evidence existed that proved Thomas didn't kill Anna—if they could find it. Without a doubt, the sheriff was involved in the crime and the coverup, but that didn't mean every deputy on the force was also involved. The problem was that she couldn't determine which deputies were and weren't. She simply couldn't risk pleading her case to the wrong person—both she and Thomas would end up behind bars.

She stared at the courthouse as if, with enough intensity, she might be able to penetrate the brick walls and see for herself what was happening inside. Several patrol cars had returned, the deputies walking in together, talking. None had come out. And neither had Thomas.

A black cat darted down the street toward her and she realized Familiar had returned. The cat's tail was fuzzed out like a Halloween caricature. He jumped into her arms and nuzzled her cheek. Before she could react, he was on the ground, tugging at her pants leg with his claws.

As the sun began to drop below the horizon, the real bitter chill of the wind picked up. Molly felt her fingers freezing and she eased away from the tree. It was time to do something.

If her gut instinct about Rachel Alain was correct—if Rachel knew about Kate and if Rachel had been trying to help Anna—then Molly needed to search the Alain house. Rachel might have left some clues that would lead to Kate's whereabouts. Molly realized she was operating on several big ifs, but she had nowhere else to turn at the moment.

She thought through the events of Rachel's murder. Rachel was killed while jogging, so the Alain home wasn't a crime scene. There was a chance that Bradley would be there. If she could catch him alone, talk to him, perhaps she could convince him that she hadn't harmed Rachel. She hadn't really tried hard to talk to the lawyer to make him see she was innocent. The shock of Rachel's murder had been so confusing she'd simply fled. To stay had been too dangerous. Now, though, with Thomas in the courthouse, likely in jail, she had little hope of resolving anything on her own. It might be best to throw herself on Bradley's mercy and try to make him believe she hadn't harmed his wife.

At least his house would be heated. She was freezing. Familiar led the way to the car, and she followed, hoping that somehow she'd find the words to make the lawyer understand that she was innocent.

The last colors of daylight were fading from the sky when she once again entered the quiet neighborhood where Bradley lived. The road, canopied with oaks, had little traffic, and she parked a block down the street, watching. There were deputies at the house. Brown-uniformed men stood in the cold, guarding the house, acting like something was going on.

Familiar watched with interest, his green gaze taking everything in. Molly gripped the steering wheel. None of this made sense. Rachel had been killed while jogging. Had someone attacked Bradley? If that was the case and he could identify his assailant, maybe he would listen to her and believe that she hadn't harmed Rachel. She knew she was grasping at straws, but she needed an ally, someone with enough power to help her free Thomas.

"Meow." Familiar looked at her, as if he read her thoughts. He nudged her elbow with his head.

She sighed. Familiar was right. "We started out on this just the two of us," she said, "and it looks like we're going to have to conclude it on our own."

Molly drove at a moderate pace down the street. It was lucky for her Miss Lily had switched car tags on the vehicle, just in case one of the deputies called it in.

As she passed the house, she noticed the

lawyer's truck was nowhere in sight, and Molly wondered if she'd been foolish to believe he'd consider talking to her. Maybe it would be best to leave. There were too many deputies around the house. Each moment she lingered was a risk. But she had to find out what had happened at the Alain house.

She pulled into a wide, curved driveway of a house a half mile away and stopped. "I'm going back on foot," she told Familiar. "If they arrest me, try to help Thomas."

She got out of the car and darted into the shadows of several dense trees. As she waited for complete darkness to fall, she remembered a million details about Rachel, the way her hair was pulled back in a ponytail for her run, the wear on her running shoes, the scattering of freckles across her cheeks and chest that told of someone who loved the outdoors. Mixed in with all of that was something else. Something that niggled at Molly's mind. Something she couldn't put her finger on.

Three men in white coats came out of the house, followed by men carrying a stretcher covered with sheets. A cold chill touched her spine. It was a body. Rachel's body. She hadn't been killed jogging. She'd been killed in her own home—perfectly framing Molly to take the fall for it.

Molly hadn't known the woman—was barely acquainted—but she keenly felt the senselessness of Rachel's death.

For fifteen minutes Molly waited as the forensic team packed up and left. Most of the deputies followed, but two stayed behind, standing in the front yard and talking quietly. When a couple of detectives came out and lit cigarettes while they chatted with the deputies, Molly saw her opportunity to dart across the Alain lawn. She flattened herself against the house, her heart pounding.

She wasn't close enough to distinguish the words of the law officers, but she could hear the murmur of their voices. She moved carefully around the house, trying one window after another. None budged. They were firmly shut.

She'd made her way almost to the front of the house. She could hear the deputies now.

"The sheriff is going to interview Lakeman as soon as he gets back to the courthouse. By the time Johnson finishes with him, Lakeman will confess to everything he did."

"I'd like to hear that," another deputy

said. "The sheriff is downtown with Mr. Alain right now, but they should be finished within the hour."

Molly could feel the hammer of her heart in her chest. She closed her eyes briefly and tried to think what to do. Before she could come up with anything, she heard one of the men.

"Do you think Alain owns a cat?" the detective asked. "That one acts like he belongs in the house."

"Bradley wouldn't have a cat, but it might be Mrs. Alain's."

"Should we let it in?" the deputy asked. "Mr. Alain didn't want to be here until we removed the body and I'm afraid maybe we accidentally let it out while we were working the crime scene."

"The dang cat's about to claw the door down. I think it lives here, and I'm letting it back inside."

Molly leaned back, letting the house support her for a moment as she took a deep breath and thanked her lucky stars that Familiar was such a terrific actor.

She held her breath as the scene played out. One of the detectives must have opened the door, and Familiar ran in the opposite direction. She could hear a hubbub of comments.

"Hey!" She heard one deputy say. "Catch him!"

She peeked around the corner of the house and saw all the lawmen engaged in trying to capture Familiar. He was darting and weaving between their legs, creating ultimate chaos. It was the only chance she'd have. She slipped behind the azaleas that bordered the front of the house to the wide-open front door and stepped into the house.

She was inside, but she had to hurry. If there was something to be found among Rachel Alain's things, she had to do it and get out. She moved back to the sitting room where she'd talked to Rachel.

Rachel had been about to go jogging. In fact, she was almost walking out the door when Molly had arrived. The common-sense presumption would be that Rachel would follow through with her jogging plans once Molly left. But she hadn't. She'd stayed home for a killer to break in and kill her.

What had changed her plans? Someone had to have been watching the house, waiting for an opportunity. Because Rachel had known something.

Moving through the house, Molly was acutely aware of the violation she was committing. She was snooping through a dead woman's things. But she had no choice. Rachel had kept a secret that had cost her her life. Molly knew that as surely as she knew her own name. It was what Rachel *didn't* tell that killed her. It was most likely what Anna *might have* told that got her killed. And Kate abducted.

And why had Bradley Alain lied about the place his wife was killed? It didn't make sense at all, unless the lie was constructed to put Molly in line as the prime suspect.

A cloud of worry for Thomas descended on her. She'd turned the cell phone tucked in the waistband of her jeans to vibrate, so she knew he hadn't tried to call her. What was happening to him? She moved through the den, her eyes adjusting to the dim lighting of the room so that she could distinguish the furniture.

Her mind seemed to dart in a dozen different directions as she avoided looking at the photograph of Anna and Kate. At last she forced herself to pick it up, to truly examine her dead sister's smiling face, to look at the innocence of the baby. Anna was dead and Kate was gone. If Molly didn't find Kate, they would both be gone from her life forever. That was unacceptable.

In the photograph, Anna and Rachel wore jogging clothes. They both looked as if they'd just finished exercising, their cheeks flushed with exertion and their hair windblown. Kate was smiling, a happy baby. Molly studied the photo more closely. It was just a snapshot, something taken as a memento for a day of fun and pleasure. There was a hint of sadness in Rachel's eyes as she looked at the camera. It made Molly feel sad, too. Anna and Rachel had been friends, and now both were dead.

"Good photograph, isn't it?"

Bradley Alain's voice chilled her to the bone. She turned to see him standing in the doorway.

"I came to talk to you." She couldn't help that her voice faltered. "I had to talk to you. Thomas is in trouble."

"Unless you're here to confess to killing my wife, I have nothing to say to you." His voice was stony.

"I didn't kill Rachel and you know it." He showed nothing of his emotions. Not even sadness at the loss of his wife.

"You were the last to see her alive."

"Except for the killer." They were speaking as if it were a lunch menu they discussed. It was one of the most horrifying conversations she'd ever heard.

"The police believe you killed her." He stood completely still, the tiniest smile at the corner of his lips. "You were the last one to see her."

"Because you've made them believe that?" She asked a question, but she knew the answer. Too many things were beginning to add up. Cold fingers of fear touch her spine.

"I do have some influence with the law." Bradley's smile widened. "It's rather useful at times."

"Rachel was killed while jogging, wasn't she? The killer brought her body back here. You and the sheriff are manipulating the murder scene to frame me."

"I hardly think that's necessary, Molly. You've managed to do a wonderful job of implicating yourself in Thomas's jailbreak and Darwin's murder. That should be plenty to send you to death row."

"Where's Thomas?"

"Locked up in jail, where he belongs. But don't worry. You'll be with him soon. The two of you, together. At least until the state puts the needles in your arms."

It was a graphic image designed to unnerve her, but as far as she could see, Bradley was unarmed. She still had a chance to get away from him.

He turned on the light in the room and walked to a telephone. "I think I'll give Paul a call. Tell him you're here."

Molly saw what he was wearing, a hunter-green fleece jacket. She remembered the tuft of material Familiar had snagged off the man who attacked Thomas. Lou Dial had managed to trace a number of jacket purchases, but the one that stuck in her head was the one Anna had bought. It wasn't merely coincidence. Anna had purchased the jacket for Bradley Alain, a gift because he was her friend's husband—or because he was Anna's lover.

She was more frightened than she'd ever been, but there was nothing for it but to bluff. "You can call the sheriff. Thomas and I are innocent. We haven't harmed anyone."

"Innocence and guilt are not always elements of the criminal justice system in this country. Surely you aren't so naive that you believed they were."

"I may have been innocent and naive a week ago, but that's no longer the case." She forced her shoulders to relax. If she ever showed her fear, he'd be relentless. "Where's Katie? Where's my niece?"

"Actually, at this point in time, I have no idea where she is."

"But she is alive."

He considered. "You should have left it alone, Molly. Both you and Thomas."

"Katie is your daughter." She held him with her gaze.

"Bravo, Molly. You put the puzzle together. How?"

This was where she could save herself or hand Alain control of her fate. She had to be as devious as he was. "My sister left a journal. I found it sewn into the mattress of Kate's bed. But you know that. You came into Anna's house to get that journal." She was hitting home. Though he was good at disguising his feelings, he couldn't deny this. The corners of his mouth had tightened. Rage? Worry? She couldn't tell, but she knew that since she had the advantage she had to press it.

"I sent that journal to a friend. If anything happens to me, she'll take it to the authorities. Thomas is in jail. You can't use him as a scapegoat for my death. And even if Sheriff Johnson is on your payroll, he's going to have to do something. I mean, Anna, Darwin, Rachel, then my sudden death—it's getting too close to home, Bradley."

Red spots had appeared in his cheeks. He was furious. Even his posture had changed.

"Your sister was an ungrateful witch, just like you. I did everything for her. I put money in her bank account so she could start a new life. I wanted her to take Katie and move away. But she wouldn't. She got greedy, and she wanted me to leave Rachel and go with her and Kate."

Molly heard something in the dining room, a scratching sound followed by the crash of something glass. Familiar was in the house, and she allowed herself one tiny smile. If she was ever going to best Bradley Alain, it would be because of Familiar.

"Who's in the house?" he demanded.

Though she was terrified, she forced her smile to widen. "A friend. I wasn't stupid enough to come here alone. But I have more questions. From that photograph, it looks like Anna and Rachel were good friends. I wonder how that's so if you were betraying your wife for Anna?"

He ignored her, his attention focused on the doorway. "Who's out there?"

"If I'm well and truly caught, humor me." Her situation was precarious, she knew that. But she couldn't give up this opportunity to find Kate. If anyone knew where she was, it was Bradley. She had no doubt that he'd engineered Anna's murder and Kate's abduction. But why? "What did Anna do that warranted killing her?"

"I'd love to indulge in your game of curiosity, but I have some loose ends to tie up. You're correct that I can't kill you here while Thomas is in jail. I guess I'm going to have to arrange another jailbreak."

He stepped closer, and Molly faltered and stepped back, brushing against one of the leather sofas. Molly could hear her heart in her ears.

"Why did you kill Rachel?"

"She couldn't keep her mouth shut. That's a deadly flaw in a wife. She was privy to too many of my secrets. After your visit, she called me. She'd begun to put it all together. She confronted me. She'd finally begun to see the bigger picture involving the babies and she said she was going to tell." He took another step forward. "I found this." He pulled the voice synthesizer from his pocket and set it on the end table. "I realized the extent of her meddling. I knew where she jogged, where she would be alone." He shrugged. "My men are very efficient."

Molly felt the sofa behind her. There was nowhere else for her to go. She was stuck.

He was closer, now about ten feet away. Molly glanced at the doorway. His hand went into his jacket and came out with a gun. He pointed it directly at her. She'd never seen such a dark, dangerous bore, and it looked as if it was pointed directly between her eyes.

"Call you friend in here," he said.

"I was bluffing. I came alone."

"I'm going to ask you one more time. Who's in this house? If you don't tell me, then I'll kill you, find whoever it is and kill them, too. There's too much at stake here to allow a nosy woman and a misguided computer geek to mess it up."

"I didn't bring anyone. Who would I ask to come? Thomas is in jail, you said. There's no one else. You know that. You designed it that way."

"You were a convenience. Once you showed up on the scene and broke Thomas out of jail, I had the perfect opportunity to kill Darwin. He was a loose cannon."

Molly had to hand it to him. Bradley Alain was a smart man. But there had to be something more behind this than one illegitimate child. Anna could have told everyone in town that Bradley was the father of Kate. That wouldn't necessitate killing her. Bradley was hiding something else—bigger stakes. And he still hadn't told her what had happened to Kate.

"Where is Katie?" She tried again. "Just tell me that."

He laughed. "If I told you that, I'd have to kill you. Then again, I'm going to kill you anyway. And your friend. Somehow I'll convince the officers outside that this was a case of breaking and entering by a deranged killer. It'll take a bit more work to get rid of Thomas, but I'm sure I can manage it." He cocked the hammer on the gun.

Familiar flew through the open doorway as if he'd been launched. He struck Bradley in the side of the head with such force that it spun the lawyer around. The gun wavered and pointed at the wall.

Molly seized the moment. She picked up the lamp beside the sofa and swung it like a bat. She caught the lawyer on the opposite side of the head. He went down hard, knocking his temple on the corner of the end table.

He gave one groan as Molly stepped over him. "Come on, Familiar. We've got to get out of here." If Bradley Alain was dead, she might never find Kate. If he was alive, he would certainly kill her the next opportunity he got. She had no choice but to get away.

## Chapter Seventeen

I managed to convince Molly to hide out while I cruised the courthouse to find out what's happening with Thomas. He's in a real pickle here. Sheriff Johnson has him sitting in a chair, handcuffed to the table. They're trying to sweat Molly's location out of him. To give him credit, he'd rather eat nails than tell them anything that might negatively impact Molly. The good news is that means Bradley hasn't regained consciousness and called his partner in crime or else they'd know where Molly had been.

The bad news is that she's out in the dark alone, and if Bradley is alive, he's surely going to be looking for her.

I've been giving this whole set of murders some thought. I feel we've seen several of the players, but I'm not sure which one is the brains, the lawyer or the sheriff. And I still don't know why they've murdered three people *just to abduct a baby that no one seems to have. There's something we haven't uncovered.*

*Tucked away in a corner of the sheriff's office where no one has noticed me yet, I've had ample opportunity to observe Sheriff Johnson. He's got the lean good looks and the badge, but he isn't the sharpest knife in the drawer. Hollywood could write better lines for him.*

*Criticizing the sheriff isn't my job. I need to figure out how to free Thomas and find proof to show that Thomas and Molly are innocent of any wrongdoing.*

*The events of the night that Anna was killed have become crystal clear to me. Anna confronted Bradley about Kate. She threatened to go public about their affair if he didn't leave his wife and marry her. He refused and likely threatened her because he couldn't afford public scrutiny. Anna couldn't go home so she went to Thomas's house, where she assumed she'd be safe. Bradley followed her there. Thinking he'd come to make up, she let him in, only to realize he meant to kill her. She ran to the bedroom and got Thomas's gun. Bradley managed to get the gun away from her and kill her. Then he took his daughter and left.*

*But what did he do with Kate?*

*That's the part where I have no answers.*

*The first order of business now is to free Thomas. If those two young deputies will only go take a cigarette break, or a bathroom break, or if I can get Thomas's eye and make him understand I need a diversion to get out of here, I'll go do some investigating on my own.*

*And where I intend to go is right here in the courthouse. A baby can't just appear out of nowhere. There will have to be records with the county courts. If someone local has Katie, there will be documentation. False records, but records. And where there's a paper trail, this feline can follow.*

THOMAS SHIFTED in the straight-backed chair. He was getting under Sheriff Johnson's skin, which was somewhat interesting and more than a little gratifying, but it wasn't getting him any closer to pulling himself out of the mess he was in. Johnson had caught him, and the sheriff acted as if he were personally going to sit on Thomas's lap until he was tried, convicted of murder and put to death.

"I want to call my lawyer," Thomas insisted.

"The law says you get a call. It doesn't say when." Johnson grinned at him. "I'm sure

Bradley will be glad to hear from you, especially since he thinks your girlfriend killed his wife." His grin widened.

Familiar shifted in his cubbyhole at the corner of a filing cabinet. Thomas saw the cat glance to the door and back to him. Familiar needed to get out of the office. He had something to do, and Thomas knew exactly how to create a diversion so the cat could make his escape.

"Lakeman, you're going to tell us where Molly Harper is." Johnson leaned so close Thomas could see the pores in his nose.

"I can't tell you because I don't know."

"What were her plans?"

"She said something about a pedicure." That answer sent the flush of high blood pressure into Johnson's cheeks, Thomas saw with satisfaction.

"You're a wiseacre now, but you won't be for long." The sheriff got up and began to pace the office. "We have you dead to rights."

Thomas had a little trick of his own. "Sheriff, when you ran the prints you lifted from Anna's neck, there wasn't a match with mine, was there?"

Johnson stopped pacing and swung around to face Thomas. "How did you—"

He broke off and looked at the two deputies guarding the door.

It was too late for him to deny it. Thomas saw the deputies exchange looks. Johnson saw it, too.

"Sheriff, I'm in the best place I can be. I have the photograph that shows the prints on Anna's neck. I also have the lab report that shows those prints don't match mine. You can go through your stack of papers there and you'll see that those two pieces of evidence are missing. They're my protection, as it were. My question here is, did the prints match someone else? Someone you're covering for?"

Johnson leaned forward. "You don't know how much trouble you're in. Making false accusations is only going to make it worse for you, so I'd shut up. Or maybe I'll shut you up."

The two deputies stepped into the room; both of them looked at each other and then at the sheriff. When Thomas looked back at the corner by the filing cabinet, Familiar was gone. He was just that quick and that stealthy. No one had even noticed him.

"We'll take the prisoner," one deputy said. "Sheriff, you should go home and get some rest. You've been on this investigation for better than a week without sleep. You're liable to do something rash if you don't get some shut-eye."

Thomas could see that all Johnson really wanted was to be alone with him somewhere in the wilderness for a few minutes. Thomas knew the sheriff wouldn't hesitate to kill him if he got the chance.

The deputies unlocked the handcuffs and stood Thomas up. One on each side, they began to escort him to the holding cell where he would stay until he was processed into the jail system.

"Look, I need one of you to pick up that report about the fingerprints."

"If you think we got you out of there because we wanted to help you, you're sadly mistaken," one deputy said. His nametag read Doug Jones.

"Deputy Jones, I'm innocent of any crime. I have evidence that can prove I didn't kill Anna Goodman. But unless you turn me loose, I can't go and get it."

"You'll get your chance in court."

"That will be too late. Sheriff Johnson will destroy the evidence, just as he's done in the past."

"That sounds like a personal problem," Jones said as he prodded Thomas forward.

"It's a problem of justice." Thomas balked. "What would it hurt to get the evidence?"

"Call your lawyer. I'm sure you're paying enough for his services. He shouldn't mind running your errands."

"I don't have a lawyer. You heard what the sheriff said. Bradley Alain won't be representing me. I doubt any lawyer in the state will."

"Another personal problem," Jones said.

Thomas shook his head, hiding his reaction. "I didn't kill Anna or Darwin Goodman. Get that fingerprint report and I'll prove it. If you don't want to believe me, you can talk to your own forensics people. They could give you a duplicate of the report."

"How'd you get that report anyway?" Jones asked.

"I stole it. If you want to prosecute me for theft, you have a case. But not murder."

The deputies hesitated. "What would it hurt to get a duplicate of the report?" Jones asked his partner. "Lately the sheriff has been kind of…"

"Nothing but a waste of our time," the other responded. "But if you're determined to do it, go ahead. I'll put him in the holding cell while I'm waiting for you to get back."

Jones stepped away from them, walking fast down the empty corridor.

"Let's get moving," the other deputy said. "I'll have you behind bars by the time he gets back from Records. Those people are disorganized. There's nobody there at night and they don't keep paperwork in any type of order."

It was the opportunity Thomas knew he had to take. He used his elbow to strike the deputy in the chest. He hit hard enough to wind the fellow. Then he used both fists on the back of the man's head to drive him to his knees. As Thomas watched, the deputy fell into the corridor unconscious.

"Sorry," Thomas said as he took the key to the handcuffs, jumped over the body of the unconscious man and ran to the front door and freedom.

MOLLY SLOWED and pulled into the alley behind Bradley Alain's office. There had to be some record of where Bradley had taken Katie. He was a stone-cold killer, and he would kill her without twitching a finger.

She kept one eye on the rearview mirror,

expecting to see blue lights flashing. Behind her was only blackness. She hoped Bradley had been knocked unconscious and that he stayed that way until she could get Thomas and provide the sheriff with the evidence necessary to prove both of them innocent.

Thomas was somewhere in the courthouse or jail. She'd helped to break him out once—unwittingly. She could do it again with intent. And she would. She'd let Familiar out at the courthouse, figuring the cat might be able to help Thomas escape. She had to free him, and she wasn't leaving Jefferson again without knowing where Kate was and how to find her. If Bradley wouldn't tell her, she meant to find it out another way.

The small town was quiet as she got out of the car and slipped to the street. She looked in both directions. There wasn't a car in sight. The cold, February night had settled over the little town snugged next to the Cypress River that looked more like Louisiana than Texas. Under different circumstances, she might want to live here.

She went back to the car and got the tire tool and a crowbar. This was a simple operation of breaking and entering. She knew exactly what she wanted from Bradley's office. She'd seen it when she visited him with Thomas.

The lawyer's office was undoubtedly rigged with cameras and alarms and any number of antitheft devices, but she didn't care if she was caught on videotape. At this point she had nothing to lose. Bradley would kill her as soon as he saw her.

She used the crowbar to break the elegant front doors and ran up the stairs to his private office. Any alarms must be silent ones, but she was counting on the fact that most of the sheriff's department had been involved in Rachel's murder. The deputies would respond, but not as quickly as normal.

She'd never considered herself particularly strong, but the rush of adrenaline gave her the power to smash the old-fashioned lock on the door to Bradley's private office. In a corner of the room near a cluster of potted plants, she saw the laptop computer. There was no guarantee that Bradley kept records on it, but she didn't have time to make copies of the files on his desktop computer, and it stood to reason that he wouldn't keep illegal records on a machine others could access. The laptop was her best choice. She picked it up and left the way she'd come.

When she pulled the car into the street, she could see a commotion at the courthouse. She kept her headlights off as she drove quickly away. She made sure no one followed as she went to the one place she felt no one would look for her.

Anna's house wasn't far from the court-house, and Molly parked down the block from the house. She wanted a change of clothes and something for Thomas to wear as well as some things for Kate. Her niece was alive, and when she found her she'd need blankets and supplies.

As soon as Thomas got out of the court-house, he could examine the laptop she'd taken from Bradley's office. Somehow, someway they'd figure it all out and find Kate.

On her way to the bedroom, Molly stopped to look at the painting she'd given Anna. It was one of her first efforts, and it clearly showed. Still, she liked the picture and had been flattered that Anna had asked to have it.

As she moved her flashlight beam over the painting, she stopped. The painting had been changed. She almost couldn't believe it, but it was true. Anna had left a clue for her—exactly the kind of clue she'd left when they were children. She'd put it in the one place she thought Molly, and no one else, would look.

Molly had originally depicted the trial of Geronimo with only adults. Now she saw that children had been added to the painting. Children wearing clothing that was incompatible with the original painting. She looked more closely. Anna had left her this clue, and wherever it led would give her the secret that Bradley Alain had killed to protect.

She grabbed up some clothes and the computer and ran to the car.

*THE RECORDS DEPARTMENT in the births and deaths system is a big mess, but I think I've hit pay dirt. According to these records, a childless couple named Darcy came in and registered a baby girl about a week ago. While this may not seem like a worthwhile avenue to investigate, I did a little bit of math and discovered that Cora and Kevin Darcy are in their fifties. Not unheard of for an adoption, but getting to be big news if it's a natural birth. The giveaway is that the baby isn't listed as adopted. This tells me that we're on the trail of Kate.*

*I could berate myself for not thinking of these records sooner, but I won't. We haven't been around Jefferson to look at the records.*

*And, I think we've stumbled onto something far bigger than Kate's abduction.*

*I'm going to tear this page out of the records book and take it to Molly and Thomas. I'll make them see the significance. We can track down the Darcys, check on the baby, and then maybe they can tell us what we need to know.*

*It was easy enough to get into this records room, but I've got to skedaddle. I hear stomping around out there. It's one of the deputies who was guarding Thomas. He's coming in here. And he's conveniently opened the door for me to make my escape. There are times—rare times—when I think how nice it would be to have a prehensile thumb. And then I remember how elegant, fleet, smart, handsome and otherwise superior I am to bipeds. Nah! I would rather be a cat.*

THOMAS SLAMMED into the front door of the courthouse and was momentarily stunned when it didn't open. He'd been moving so fast he hit with enough force to rattle the old door on its hinges. But it held. He'd been hiding in a supply closet in the courthouse, waiting for a chance to get out.

When his escape had first been reported, deputies had swarmed everywhere. Now, though, something else had drawn them from the building. He had to make his escape fast, but he was locked in.

There was no sound of pursuit behind him. Thomas had no doubt that by now Deputy Jones had returned from the records room and found his partner unconscious on the floor and Thomas gone again. The general alarm had been sounded. It was only a matter of minutes before the deputies would consider that Thomas was still in the courthouse. For this escape, Thomas didn't have an accomplice. No black cat detective to help him out. Familiar was probably long gone into the night by now.

"Meow!"

Whirling around, Thomas almost stepped on Familiar. The cat had one paw on a sheet of paper. Thomas bent down to scoop both of them up.

"Am I glad to see you," he said as he put the cat back on the floor. "Find us a way out."

Familiar grabbed at his pants leg and then ran down a corridor and disappeared into what looked like a men's room. Thomas didn't hesitate. He followed.

When he got into the men's bathroom, Thomas didn't see a sign of the cat.

"Familiar?"

He heard the meow and followed the noise to the last booth. Thomas could only shake his head in amazement. Obviously a plumber had been called in to work on some of the pipes. In doing so, he'd removed the back wall of one of the stalls. The open space led to a corridor and a door to a loading dock. Familiar waited for Thomas on the dock, his black tail twitching in the glow from a floodlight.

"Let's make tracks." Thomas matched his stride to Familiar's, and the two of them sprinted across the courthouse lawn and into the street.

Thomas saw the car's headlights just as Familiar sprang from the curb. Thomas was moving too fast to stop. He leaned down and pulled the cat to him as his legs churned in an effort to clear the path of the car.

## Chapter Eighteen

Molly slammed on the brakes and was thrown against the seat belt with enough force to lose her breath. Her sharp cry of fright mingled with the sounds of the tires grabbing the pavement as the car went into a sideways slide.

Telephone poles whizzed by, but Molly didn't feel the thud that would have meant she'd hit the man running into the street. She brought the car to a complete stop headed in the direction she'd come from. She was so frightened—and so angry—that she got out of the car without thinking. As the man picked himself up out of the road, a black cat jumped from his arms.

Molly stopped in her tracks. She stared at the cat, then the man, and then she gave a cry of relief. Her knees began to buckle, but Thomas was right there beside her. His strong hand, a little bloodied by his scrape along the pavement, caught her elbow and held her upright.

"Good timing," he said as he urged her back toward the car. Familiar scampered along beside him. "We've got to get out of here before all hell breaks loose."

"You don't know the half of it." She got behind the wheel. She held back all her questions and revelations until they were on the road. She drove blindly—and with speed. It didn't matter where they went. There was no place left to hide, unless she could prove her suspicions.

Familiar hopped into the front seat and began to head-butt Molly's elbow, a gesture to show how glad he was that she was okay.

"So much has happened," Molly said at last. "Bradley killed Anna and his wife. He admitted it. I think he paid someone to kill Darwin."

"The sheriff is in it with him, whatever it is."

"Meow!" Familiar patted Thomas pocket where he'd put the piece of paper.

"What's Familiar telling us?" she asked.

"Familiar found this. It's a record of a birth, a daughter named Emily Ann born to Cora and Kevin Darcy." With Familiar's prompting, Thomas got out a pen and began to do some calculations. In a moment he added, "A couple in their fifties. This isn't a natural birth, but it isn't listed as an adoption."

"Kate!" Molly knew it. That small tidbit confirmed everything she'd begun to believe about Bradley Alain.

Thomas touched her arm. "I think it is Kate, but remember, we have to survive to be able to find her. Bradley and the sheriff will surely kill us if they can. They can't afford to let us live."

"I know." Molly only wanted to sink into his arms, even if it was just for a moment. Thomas made her feel safe, protected. He stood between her and the danger that seemed to rise up from all fronts. He gave her strength. "Bradley tried to kill me earlier, but I used his head for batting practice with a lamp." She saw the ghost of Thomas's smile.

"I hope you hit a homer."

"Pretty close. He fell and struck his head on the end table. He was breathing when I left, but I didn't hang around to administer first aid."

"I hope he's able to talk." He rubbed her arm. "You're shaking. Why don't you pull over and let me drive?"

As soon as Molly stopped, he got out of the car and walked around.

When she was in the passenger's seat, he turned the car around and headed back toward town. "Where are we going?" she asked.

"Back to Bradley's house. I'm tired of running. I'm tired of defending myself against charges that aren't true, of seeing the people I love put through the wringer. If that creep is alive, I'm going to get the truth out."

"That may not be necessary," Molly said.

Thomas slowed the car. "Why not?"

"I stole his laptop computer. We may be able to find all the evidence we need right there. You can find it, Thomas. You have the skill to do it."

This time Thomas's grin was earsplitting. "That's the best news I've heard in a long time, but a little disappointing."

"Why?" Molly couldn't believe it.

"I was really looking forward to smashing my fist into Bradley's face over and over again. Now we may not have to."

"Oh, I think we'll arrange a little session of fisticuffs just for the two of you, but after we have the evidence we need. I want to go get Kate, and I don't want this hanging over my head when I do."

"Meow!" Familiar agreed.

THE PATH THOMAS CHOSE was dirt, and the car bumped over it as he pulled a half mile off the main road. They were in the middle of a pasture with only the stars and a few cows for company. They couldn't evade the law forever, but this might give him time to break into the computer.

"You can do it." Molly's voice held total confidence. She caressed his face with her fingertips. "Let's put Bradley Alain behind bars where he belongs."

Thomas got the plug that converted the cigarette lighter to a computer connection and turned it on. In a moment he had the menus up. He started to work, tripping layer after layer of security codes and walls. He worked on instinct, and with a knowledge of how Bradley Alain's mind worked. Bradley was a man without any scruples, yet he pretended to love his wife and maintained a fiction about his existence. A man like that would repeat that pattern in many aspects of his life, including his pass codes and protections.

Thomas kept working. He wasn't going to get into a car race with the police. He wouldn't risk Molly's life. The answer was right in front of them, if he could just get into the computer.

"Dammit!" He struck the dash with his fist. "I'm almost in, but I can't figure out how to get past this one wall."

"Meow." Familiar hopped onto the console. He walked over to Thomas and rubbed his head against his chin.

"Later, Familiar." Thomas tried to push the cat away, but Familiar wasn't taking no for an answer. "What?"

Familiar batted the paper he'd brought from the courthouse. "We're going to go see the Darcys to-morrow, but I need the password now."

"Meow!" Familiar tried again.

"What does he want?" Thomas asked Molly in exasperation.

"He's trying to tell us something. I think…" She grabbed Thomas's hand. "It's the password. Try Kate!"

His fingers flying, Thomas typed in the four letters. The password was denied.

"It has to relate somehow to Kate. Maybe Anna?"

Thomas tried again, again without success.

"If it has to do with Kate…" Thomas felt as if his brain had frozen. "Stolen, kidnapped…" He tried both of those words without success. "What?" Any minute the law would find them and he wouldn't have another chance. Bradley would take the computer, and that would be the end of it.

"When I was in Anna's house, she'd changed a painting I'd done. She painted in children."

"Meow!" Familiar cried.

Molly gripped Thomas's shoulder. "Adoption! That's the word. That's what Bradley's been doing—selling children to adoptive parents!"

Thomas keyed in the word. He was in!

IT'S ABOUT TIME *someone listened to me. I figured out a long time ago that Kate was the ticket to unlock this mystery. Uh-oh. I hear sirens, and they seem to be drawing closer to us. I wonder how they followed us.*

*Not hard to figure out, now that a helicopter is spotlighting us. Thomas is still busy at the keyboard. He's found what he's looking for. Good Lord. It's a list of children, maybe thirty or forty. They're listed as "unknown origin" which translates into "stolen." That bum Bradley Alain is going down, and I want to be there when it happens.*

DEPUTY DOUG JONES led the deputies toward the car. Thomas got out with his hands up. "Get out slowly," Thomas warned Molly. He had to yell to be heard over the noise of the helicopter. "These guys aren't very happy with either of us."

"You're under arrest," Jones said. In the glare of the chopper's lights, his face was red and angry. Thomas had played him for a fool, but under his anger, Thomas was counting on Jones to be a rational man.

"We understand." Thomas put his hands on the car. "Molly," he yelled to her. "Don't move suddenly." He looked around to see that Familiar stood on the dash, watching.

"Where's the sheriff?" Thomas asked as the deputies searched him for a weapon. He let his arms go limp as they put the cuffs on him. It hurt him to see Molly being handcuffed, but now wasn't the time to complain. The deputy in charge of Molly moved her to the waiting patrol car. He watched as they deposited Molly into the back.

"Sheriff's waiting at the courthouse."

"Did you get those records?" Thomas asked.

"What if I did?" Jones grabbed him by the shoulder and pushed him toward the waiting patrol car. Overhead, the chopper moved away.

With the noise level diminished, Thomas had an opportunity to talk to Jones before they joined the other deputies.

"There's a computer in the car," he said, urgency threaded through his voice. "It belongs to Bradley Alain. He's involved in stealing children in third-world countries and selling them. He's taking them from people who can't fight back. Poor people. He was behind the murder of Anna Goodman and the disap-pearance of the baby Kate. He killed Darwin, who must have been involved in the scheme somehow, and then he killed his wife when she decided to tell Molly the truth about Kate's whereabouts. You have to believe me."

"You're not exactly in a position to tell me what I have to do," Jones said, but there was doubt in his voice.

"Think about it, man. You know the sheriff is involved in this. You know it in your gut. If you take me and Molly back there without checking into this, you're delivering us into the hands of the men who will kill us."

Jones hesitated. "You've got a big mouth and a lot of wild theories. That's all you've got."

"You got those records. Look at them. Johnson has manipulated every piece of evidence. He's used you and your partners to help him commit crimes. I have copies of the reports in the car. Just look at them. Look at the fingerprint report. I didn't kill Anna Goodman."

At the sound of the cat's angry yowl, Thomas and the deputy turned. Familiar darted out of the car with the photograph of Anna's neck and the fingerprint report. He dropped both pieces of evidence at the deputy's feet.

"What's the holdup, Jones?" One of the deputies called out. "Bring 'im on up. You need some help?"

"Just a minute." Jones picked up the photo and report. He bent to use the headlights of the car to examine them. When he looked up at Thomas, his face clearly showed his concern. "We never saw this fingerprint report. I couldn't find it in the record room."

"Johnson is hooked up with Bradley Alain."

"You can't be certain of that."

"I am. And you are, too."

"I'm still taking you in." Jones put the photo and report inside his jacket. "Come on."

"Check the computer. The children are represented by numbers. There are thirty or thirty-five of them. It's a big operation. Some people paid tens of thousands for a child. Some people who maybe weren't qualified to adopt from a legitimate agency."

Jones pulled the computer from the car and looked at it. "I'm not sure I get all of that from this spreadsheet."

"I can show you. That's the solid proof of what I'm telling you. Whatever you have to do with me, don't let anything happen to that computer."

"If you're selling me a load of—"

"I'm not. What I said is the truth, and I can prove it. Just print out that sheet and then go to the addresses. You'll find a child that wasn't born into that family. Check Bradley's bank accounts. Check for accounts offshore. I can help you do that."

"Let's go."

"What about the cat?" Thomas asked. "You can't leave him out here to freeze."

"I've seen that black one in the courthouse." Jones was puzzled.

"Familiar will be okay in town. Just give him a ride."

Jones reached into the car and picked up Familiar. Thomas walked obediently beside him to the patrol car. When he was put in the back beside Molly, he gave her a nod of approval.

"The deputy's smart. He's thinking it through. I get the sense he's onto the sheriff, even if he doesn't want to be."

"If they leave us alone in that jail, Johnson and Bradley will figure out a way to kill us."

Thomas knew that. "Even if they do, Jones has the computer. He'll figure out what's going on. Familiar has a ride into town. He can take care of himself. Right now we've done the best we can do."

*MY JOB IS TO TAKE CARE of Miss Molly and the cowboy, and I can see I'm going to have my work cut out for me. We're headed back to the courthouse and the jail. Bradley can't afford to let Molly and Thomas live. Based on my vast experience of humanoid criminal behavior, late tonight Bradley's going to show up and arrange for a jailbreak. Only, Thomas and Molly will walk right into a barrage of bullets and death. Bradley wants them silenced.*

*So I'll play along, get into the courthouse, and then plan my defense of my humanoids. If it comes down to gunfire, I intend to make sure the only person who gets hit is the bad guy.*

THE CELL WAS FREEZING. Molly wrapped the coarse blanket around her shoulders and tried not to shiver. She couldn't be certain if it was the temperature or dread that made her teeth chatter. She'd been in the cell for two hours or better, without a peep from Thomas. She didn't know what had happened to him, but she suspected nothing good.

She tried to focus on Kate, a happy baby living with a doting older couple. Molly knew that if she died, Kate would still have a loving family. That was some solace. A little.

The courthouse had been completely silent for the past half hour. Bradley would come soon. Or his paid henchmen. John, Judy, the men who'd killed Darwin, it wouldn't matter. Bradley would have to act—he couldn't afford to let her or Thomas live. She knew it, and she wondered what she could do to stop it. Not a thing came to mind.

She heard the jangle of a key and knew it had begun. Footsteps came toward the cell.

The deputy Thomas had placed his faith in had sold them out.

The footsteps drew nearer.

"You couldn't leave it alone, could you?" Bradley stood at the bars of her cell. "I didn't want to kill you. Or Anna for that matter. But you've given me no choice."

"What about your wife? I guess Rachel didn't give you a choice, either."

"She was going to tell. She found the paperwork on Kate, and she confronted me. I thought she'd bought the story I told her, but she was smarter than I gave her credit for being. I know she sent you a note and called you. I warned her what would happen if she persisted. She said you deserved to raise your flesh and blood. I knew if you started poking around, you'd find out about the other babies."

"It's too late. One of the deputies has all the information."

"The sheriff will keep his men in line. He's well paid to do that."

"Everything is unraveling, Bradley. You know it. It's too late. You're going to be caught."

"If that's the case, then I'll kill you and Lakeman for the pleasure of it. With three other murders on my hands, what do I have to lose?"

His words made Molly's throat spasm, but she fought the sensation of illness. She had to keep her head.

Bradley unlocked the cell. "Come on out."

Molly shook her head. "No. You're going to have to kill me right here in this cell."

"That won't be a hardship." He brought a gun from beneath his jacket and pointed it at her chest.

She tasted fear as his finger tightened on the trigger.

"Drop it, Alain." Doug Jones pressed the barrel of his .357 to the lawyer's back. "This shot won't kill you, but you won't ever walk again."

"Deputy, she was trying to escape. I just—"

"Can it, Alain. We got the whole conversation on tape. Your confession, everything." Jones roughly grabbed Bradley's wrists and snapped on the cuffs. "Ms. Harper, you're free to go," he said.

When Molly exited the jail cell, Jones pushed Bradley in and slammed the door. "Now, I don't think many people will come to your aid, Alain. But you won't be lonely for long. In about ten minutes Sheriff Johnson is going to be in the cell next to you. And the men you hired to kill Darwin Goodman as well as the Adams couple. Once confronted with a list of crimes, I'm sure one of them will give us the gritty details for a reduced sentence."

Molly stepped back. She was so relieved she felt light-headed. And she faltered right into the arms of Thomas Lakeman. Familiar was at his side.

"Ms. Harper, I owe you an apology," Deputy Jones said. "Mr. Lakeman showed me the computer files. He rigged a camera to videotape Alain when he came into the cell to kill you."

"I thought he was going to succeed." Molly's head was still reeling.

"Meow!" Familiar was indignant.

"Not a chance with the black cat around. He was perched up there." Jones pointed to a ceiling tile that was loose. "If that lawyer had made another move, the cat was going to shred his head."

"I would have paid good money for that," Thomas said. He looked in the cell at Bradley. "Maybe we could do it anyway."

Jones herded all of them out of the jail. "No way. Not on my watch. Alain will be tried and convicted and he will pay for his crimes. That's how justice is supposed to work."

As they entered the sheriff's office, the

door opened and two deputies brought a struggling Paul Johnson in, his hands cuffed behind him.

Thomas put his arm around Molly and drew her close against him. Familiar hissed at the sheriff as the deputies led him back to a cell.

"We'll get the rest of them, I promise," Jones said. "I know it's late, but I think there's a little girl who might want to see her aunt. While you're driving, I'll give the Darcys a call and explain all of this. If you folks have any trouble, just pick up a phone."

Molly didn't need a second invitation to leave. She took Thomas's hand, and with a nod to Familiar they left the courthouse together.

DAWN ARRIVED PINK and cold. Molly and Thomas sat on the sofa in the Darcy house. Molly held a sleeping Kate in her arms. Thomas watched them. He'd never been prouder in his life. He'd had a hand in bringing Molly and her niece back together. He and Familiar. He stroked the black cat who'd just gorged himself on fresh cream and a lamb chop that Cora Darcy had prepared.

All in all, the Darcys had been wonderful. They'd feared that Kate belonged to someone else, someone who would want her back.

"You two are meant to be together," Cora said to Molly. "We love her so much, we can't stand between her and her blood. We're not the kind of people who would fight over a child in court. You have the legal right and the moral right. We suspected when Bradley Alain showed up with her and asked us to take her in and adopt her that something wasn't right. He said she was an unwanted ward of the court. So we took her and never spoke about our concerns."

Molly's eyes filled with tears. "There will never be a time when you won't be welcome in her life. She's going to be a lucky little girl to have me for an aunt and you two for parents."

Kevin cleared the lump from his throat. "Maybe she can come over here from Arizona during the summer. Spend a few weeks. I want to teach her to barrel ride and herd cows." He chuckled to hide the emotion behind his words. "Useful skills for every little cowgirl."

Molly ducked her head and looked at Thomas. "I don't think that will be necessary."

"Why not?" Kevin was concerned.

"I've decided to move here, to Jefferson." The smile that touched her face was luminous. "A certain cowboy-slash-computer-geek has made me an offer I can't refuse. He's letting me keep a little homeless kitten for Kate on the condition I move here."

As if she knew her name, the tiny kitten jumped onto the sofa and rubbed against Kate's feet, making the baby giggle with pleasure.

"Nothing would do for Thomas but that we stop by the shop in Jefferson and pick up the stray kitten on our way here. He was afraid she would freeze to death last night," Molly said. "She's going to be part of the family, too."

Cora burst into applause. "Congratulations! This is the best news I've had since we got little Emil—I mean, Kate."

"I thought you might want to share in her life. I can move. I'm not tied to one place, and I can continue to do my work with the artists on the reservation and live here." She reached over and touched Thomas's face. "I want to be near the man I love."

"I think I hear the sound of wedding bells," Kevin said. He went to Cora and held her hand. "The best decision I ever made in life was to ask this woman to be my wife."

Molly held up a palm. "All in good time. I

still have to grieve the death of my sister. And I need to get to know Kate. Thomas and I have the rest of our lives before us."

Thomas couldn't help himself. He leaned over and kissed Molly lightly on the lips. "I've got you corralled now, Molly Harper. There's not a chance you're going to get away from me. I'm patient, and I'll wait. But your days of roaming the range are over. Your heart belongs to me."

*I FIND MOST humanoid babies to be rather helpless, but I see a spark of intelligence in Kate's gray eyes. She's going to be a cutter. Thomas and Molly will have their hands full with her—and with the kitten.*

*Thomas hasn't popped the question to Molly yet, but my heart tells me it won't be long before those two are married and building a family unit that will be strong enough to withstand anything.*

*As Molly says, all in good time. She wants to give herself time to learn about Thomas. She feels she made a mistake in her first marriage, and she wants to take it slow. That's never a bad plan, but I could tell her— if she'd listen—that she's already left the past far behind her. Trouble with humanoids is that they have selective hearing. It would be a waste of my energy, and I'm smart enough to drop it.*

*After that wonderful breakfast prepared by Cora, I need a nap. I have a couple of hours before my flight leaves from Shreveport, Louisiana. The case is solved, the bad guys are behind bars, Kate is home where she belongs and Molly and Thomas are cleared of all charges. Not a bad week's work, if you ask me.*

*I'll curl up here and nap and dream about Clotilde, my sweet calico. Happy trails, until we meet again.*

# HARLEQUIN®
# INTRIGUE®

## WE'LL LEAVE YOU BREATHLESS!

If you've been looking for thrilling tales of
contemporary passion and sensuous love stories
with taut, edge-of-the-seat suspense—then
you'll love Harlequin Intrigue!

Every month, you'll meet six new heroes
who are guaranteed to make your spine tingle
and your pulse pound. With them you'll enter
into the exciting world of Harlequin Intrigue—
where your life is on the line
and so is your heart!

## THAT'S INTRIGUE—
## ROMANTIC SUSPENSE
## AT ITS BEST!

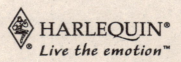

HARLEQUIN®
*Live the emotion*™

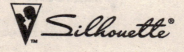

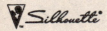

# INTIMATE MOMENTS™

*Sparked by danger, fueled by passion!*

# Passion.
# Adventure.
# Excitement.

**Enter a world that's
larger than life, where
men and women overcome
life's greatest odds for
the ultimate prize: love.
Nonstop excitement is
closer than you think...in
Silhouette Intimate Moments!**

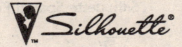

Visit Silhouette Books at www.eHarlequin.com

SIMDIR104

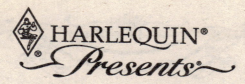

# HARLEQUIN®
## *Presents*®

**The world's bestselling romance series...**
**The series that brings you your favorite authors,**
**month after month:**

Helen Bianchin...Emma Darcy
Lynne Graham...Penny Jordan
Miranda Lee...Sandra Marton
Anne Mather...Carole Mortimer
Susan Napier...Michelle Reid

**and many more uniquely talented authors!**

Wealthy, powerful, gorgeous men...
Women who have feelings just like your own...
The stories you love, set in exotic, glamorous locations...

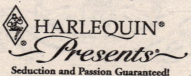

# HARLEQUIN®
## *Presents*®

**Seduction and Passion Guaranteed!**

www.eHarlequin.com

## Harlequin Historicals®
### Historical Romantic Adventure!

*From rugged lawmen and valiant knights to defiant heiresses and spirited frontierswomen, Harlequin Historicals will capture your imagination with their dramatic scope, passion and adventure.*

*Harlequin Historicals…
they're too good to miss!*

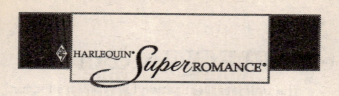

# ...there's more to the story!

**Superromance.**
A *big* satisfying read about unforgettable characters. Each month we offer *six* very different stories that range from family drama to adventure and mystery, from highly emotional stories to romantic comedies—and much more! Stories about people you'll believe in and care about. Stories too compelling to put down....

Our authors are among today's *best* romance writers. You'll find familiar names and talented newcomers. Many of them are award winners—and you'll see why!

If you want the biggest and best in romance fiction, you'll get it from Superromance!

## Emotional, Exciting, Unexpected...

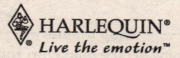

**HARLEQUIN®**
*Live the emotion*™